Alex A. Zudor

Male Parta

An Agent Strabo Mystery (#3)

Copyright @ 2021 Alex A. Zudor

All rights reserved

The characters and events portrayed in this book are fictitious. Any similarity to real persons, living or dead, is coincidental and not intended by the author.

No part of this book may be reproduced, or stored in a retrieval system, or transmitted in any form or by any means, electronic, mechanical, photocopying, recording, or otherwise, without express written permission of the publisher.

ISBN: 9798396476431

Cover design by: Ingrid Zudor
Published in the United States of America

TO MY MOTHER, LORETA AURELIA,

Thank you for everything

Table of Contents

- I. Meet the Lucretii 7
- II. A Night in the Woods 23
- III. Boys with Swords 33
- IV. A Deadly Interview 47
- V. The Good Old Doctor 63
- VI. In the Shadow of Kings 77
- VII. The Goddess of the Hunt 89
- VIII. The Name of the Enemy 99
- IX. Cupid's Stealthy Arrow 109
- X. A Fort in Disarray 119
- XI. An Offer One Can't Refuse 135
- XII. A Fiery Trap 143
- XIII. Zalmoxis Revealed 157

Ave, Lector! 171

Books by the Author 173

Agent Strabo's Roman Mysteries 177

About the Author 179

I. Meet the Lucretii

The afternoon sun warmed Strabo's face. He sat on the bench, eyes closed, listening to the sounds around him. He could hear the babbling of the nearby stream, insects buzzing, and birds chirping—early spring was his favorite season.

"Aaa!" He sighed.

He opened his eyes, taking in the equally serene view. The lush green grass dotted with white flowers, the freshly sown fields, the watermill, and the forested mountains in the background, some of the peaks still capped in snow.

"Lucius Lucretius, are you daydreaming again?" Strabo was startled by the unexpected voice.

"No, mum, I was just wondering, once again, how much I missed this place."

Although she celebrated forty last summer, Strabo's mother was still an attractive woman. Her long brown hair, common among indigenous people, was tied up in a bun. Strabo inherited her melancholy, dark eyes and full, sensual lips.

Her gaze rested on her son, embracing him in a way only a loving mother could do.

"I remember the day you joined the legions. You were so eager to leave all this behind...." She left the thought hanging.

Strabo shook his head. "Five years of war can change a man."

"Why haven't you contacted us? Not even after returning to Sarmizegetusa?"

And here it comes, Strabo thought. The question he had dreaded since he came to visit almost three months ago, right before Saturnalia, finally came up.

A year passed since he was seriously wounded in the civil war's climactic Battle of Lugdunum, losing his left eye. As a result, he had to leave Emperor Septimius' *Legio XIII Gemina*. Still, instead of returning to his father's rural *villa*, he stayed in the provincial metropolis of Ulpia Traiana Sarmizegetusa, drinking himself to an early grave.

What kept me away? He had no clear answer to that. Maybe it was the shame of being a cripple, or perhaps he just needed time to deal with the previous five years' events.

Irrespective of the reasons for not coming home, after a period of drunken misery, he encountered his former commander, Gnaeus Manlius Hilarius, one of the senior officers of the Thirteenth. Hilarius offered him a position as *frumentarius*, an agent of the Imperial secret service. It took Strabo half a year and a couple of successful cases under his belt to build up the confidence to face his parents.

"I don't know, mum. I was just…you know…"

She smiled and ruffled his hair. "It doesn't matter. We are happy you are back, safe, and sound. Now go, clean yourself up before dinner. Your father is warming the baths already."

Strabo stood up, stretched his back lazily, and walked toward the small building housing the baths.

His father was in the changing room, already naked, waiting for him. While he was much older than his mother, Strabo could see that his stocky body was as strong as on the day he was honorably discharged from the legions. His features were unmistakably Roman, although he was born here, in the province.

His father's father, another legionary veteran, hailed from Germania Inferior, a couple of thousands of miles away from Dacia. Coincidentally, his city of birth was renamed Ulpia Traiana, the same as the place he chose to retire to, the newly erected capital of the Dacia—two cities a world apart and yet so similar.

However, Strabo's great-grandfather was a pure-blooded Roman, bred and born in Latinum. Hence the aquiline nose that allowed Strabo to look down on people way taller than him and the long, bony face so familiar in the central parts of Italia.

"Come now. Your mother doesn't like us being late for dinner."

They stripped before entering the *tepidarium*, the warm room—it was large enough to fit four persons comfortably. They lounged in silence on the stone benches, enjoying the warmth. Eventually, Lucretius Ofella, Strabo's father, broke the silence.

"I assume you must go back soon, now that the winter is over."

"Yes, father. Duty calls."

"Do you mind if I ask what happened?" Ofella pointed at his son's eyepatch.

Strabo sighed. "It is a long story, father."

They sat in silence for a while, the sounds of the heating water murmuring in the background.

"Well, we have a bit of time," Ofella said eventually.

"Can we at least move on to the hot tub?"

Once they submerged into the *caldarium*'s pool, Strabo recounted his five years as a legionary. He described the marches through the Empire, the various battles and sieges, his assignment as a military intelligence operative, the epic Battle of Lugdunum, and how he lost his eye.

Ofella listened silently, then nodded. "You had quite an adventure, Lucius. So what happened then? You got a medical discharge?"

"Yep, I did. Barely an adult and already discharged." He shrugged. "Still, the gods must have loved me. I bumped into Hilarius one hazy morning, and he recruited me as a *frumentarius* despite my disheveled state." Strabo laughed out loud. "Hilarius' name be praised for all of eternity, for you know how much I hate farming."

His father joined the laughter. "I wouldn't have guessed." Offela's tone turned serious after a few heartbeats. "Still, I could take care of your land, for now, build a nice little villa, plant an orchard. These things take time, you know?"

Strabo gestured invitingly. "Be my guest, father."

"Good, we can go into town tomorrow and sort out the paperwork. Then, once you empower your old man to take care of your land, I will visit and begin the necessary preparations."

"What about your farm here?"

"Ehh, it is all routine now, and the boys know what to do." Offela grinned. "Moreover, they are too afraid of your mother to slack while I am gone." Strabo smiled, well aware of his mother's headstrong character.

"Look, son, one day you will decide to settle down. Your life will be much easier with everything up and running already. On both farms."

"Come now, father. You are in better shape than I ever was. I am confident you still have many summers ahead of you."

"One more reason to help you while I still can. Now, enough of this. Tell me about Hilarius. I remember him as a young legionary."

"He remembers you too. He said you were a good officer, but…."

Ofella raised an eyebrow: "But what?"

"Well, he wouldn't say. All he said was you haven't been promoted to senior centurion because something happened. Care to share?"

His father stepped out of the tub gesturing for Strabo to scrape his back with the strigil. Strabo suspected he did this on purpose to avoid facing his son.

"Bah, I cared too much for my men and didn't spend enough time ass-kissing."

Strabo decided to drop the subject for now. "Any regrets?"

"I am the first in the family to join the centurionate. I built a nice place for ourselves alongside a good woman that kept me honest. And...," he turned to face Strabo before continuing, "my son turned out to be a hero and made it to *optio* at only 23. What else could a Roman father wish for?"

Strabo was speechless. It was probably the first time his father showed affection toward him since he reached adulthood.

"Well, you might expect your son to surpass your achievements."

"I am a realist," Ofella said, then grinned. "Besides, you still have your whole life ahead of you." He gestured to his son. "Turn around; let us finish this before dinner gets cold and your mother kicks our asses. Take my advice and never provoke a Dacian, for even their womenfolk are dangerous."

******

A week has passed since Strabo empowered his father to manage his land. They were on the porch, planning the layout of his future *villa rustica*.

"As soon as I hire the supervisor and buy a few slaves, we must build their quarters. If we are lucky, we can even raise a shed, an animal pen, and a storehouse and plant the orchard this year. Next year we will build your house, plant the vegetable garden and prepare the fields. In three years, you might have a fully running farm and earn a profit in five. But all these things will require further investment, so try not to drink all your earnings."

Strabo smirked. "I still have half of my *praemia*. You could stop by Sarmizegetusa and withdraw the necessary amounts from the *argentarius*."

"Good…ah, here comes Titus Hortensius." Ofella stood to greet his neighbor. "*Salve, vicine!*"

"Salve," Hortensius said.

"Join us. Zina, bring another cup!"

"I see you are planning young Lucius' farm." Strabo's mother emerged from the house, bringing a wooden cup for their guest. "Thank you, Zina. By the way, have you heard the news?"

"What news?" she asked while pouring wine into Hortensius' cup.

"A few days ago, one of the boys garrisoned at the ruins up the mountains was found dead. A gruesome murder, they say. Apparently, the lad's body was pierced by several spears."

Strabo's mother knocked down the pitcher, red wine spilling on the table. "I am sorry; let me bring a kitchen towel and clean up." Zina rushed into the house.

Ofella waved his wife's concerns away. "Any suspects?"

Hortensius leaned forward and said in a hushed voice, "The body was found in the ruins of the old Dacian temple. Some say it was a human sacrifice."

Ofella bristled. "Nonsense! I was born in this province and never heard of the locals practicing human sacrifice."

Strabo interjected, "Titus Hortensius, where did you hear this news?"

"I stopped for a quick drink in the tavern yesterday while on business in town. A passing auxilia shared the story. According to this guy, the garrison's centurion dispatched a courier to Apulum, asking their auxiliary praefect how to handle the unusual situation."

As soon as the news reaches Apulum, Hilarius will hear about it, Strabo thought.

Ofella caught his son's eye and nodded his understanding. "I assume you'll leave in the early morning, son. I'll ask your mother to prepare some food for the road—as you know, it will not be an easy ride up the mountains."

"Thank you, father. I'll write Hilarius immediately. He should be aware I am heading up there to investigate."

******

Strabo woke up before dawn and prepared the equipment for the trip ahead. His father was at the stables, saddling Strabo's horse. His mother finished preparing breakfast and sat at the table, silently watching her eating son.

"Mum, I spent my whole childhood roaming these mountain woods. Please don't worry." Strabo tried to put on a reassuring face despite him being half asleep.

Zina blinked rapidly, then said, "I know Lucius, I know. It is just…." She sighed heavily, leaving the thought hanging in the air. "Just please be very careful, alright? There is more to these woods than you might think." She involuntarily took her hand to her chest, touching the wooden symbol she always wore on a leather chain around her neck.

Strabo reached out and placed his hands on her mother's. "Mum, I'll be fine, I promise. Probably it was just an ordinary murder prompted by a drunken fight or a gambling debt. Unfortunately, it happens all the time."

She was unconvinced. "I suppose you are right. Still, the spears…but it can't be. The garrison there is not drawn from the local population, right?"

He shook his head, confused. "What does this have to do with anything?"

"Are they locals or not?"

"I don't think so. The cohort is called '*I. Pannoniorum*'—I guess most soldiers are from *Pannonia*. Some are probably from Dacia and the other neighboring provinces of *Moesia* and *Thracia*, maybe even from *Illyricum* or *Macedonia*."

"I see," Zina said. "Lucius Lucretius, please promise your mother that if the dead auxiliary was a Dacian or he was from *Moesia* or *Thracia*, you'll give up the investigation."

"Why? I don't understand."

"Because there is a high chance this wasn't a murder. I can't tell you more. Just promise me."

"Mum, I am a *frumentarius*, and I can't just give up on an investigation."

"Promise me!"

"Alright, I promise I'll stop investigating if this turns out not to be murder after all. Now I need to go. The sun is up already." He stood, picked up the pouch prepared by his mother, kissed her on the cheek, and left the house.

Time to saddle up and ride.

II. A Night in the Woods

His *terminus* was the small fort guarding the ruins of the former Dacian capital, Sarmizegetusa Regia. The Romans took more than the lands from the original inhabitants; they also appropriated their capital's name.

After conquering the Dacian kingdom, Emperor Marcus Ulpius Traianus destroyed the ancient capital and built a new one circa 50 miles southwest of the former. He named the new city Ulpia Traiana Sarmizegetusa, partly after himself and partly after the original urban center he had just destroyed. Moreover, to ensure the Dacians wouldn't restore the center of their long-lost civilization, the Emperor left a small garrison to guard against any intrusion.

Traianus must have been a lovely guy.

Typically, to reach his destination, Strabo should have circled west toward his home city of Ulpia Traiana Sarmizegetusa, then gone northwards in the direction of

Apulum, and finally turned back eastwards toward the ruins of Sarmizegetusa Regia and the Roman fort guarding them. However, Strabo decided to ride directly north from his father's estate to avoid the long detour—the local herders have used the mountain paths since the dawn of time.

Initially, the ride was easy. Strabo entered a valley flanked by wooded outcrops on both sides, with a clear mountain stream trickling through the rocks. The raw-green grass on its banks was still wet, sunlight bouncing off the morning dew. White, blue, and purple mountain flowers dotted the idyllic landscape.

As the miles passed, the valley became narrower, and the forest crept closer and closer to the stream. Finally, Strabo reached a rock wall, and the only way forward was up the opening cut by the water over the millennia. He dismounted and led his horse on.

His feet froze as soon as he stepped into the ice-cold stream. Strabo struggled to keep his balance as he climbed the slippery river stones. He had to use both his hands and legs at some point, so he hooked the horse's reins to his leather belt. They went on like this for what seemed like an eternity. Eventually, a wet and exhausted Strabo emerged on the other side of the gully—a slope greeted him. The angle was too steep to ride, but at least he could walk upright.

Not before I take a break.

As the sun reached its zenith, Strabo dropped down on his back. He basked in the warm sun rays in an attempt to dry his wet clothes. His horse happily munched the fresh grass.

******

Strabo woke up to the sound of bells.

I must have dozed off.

He sat up and looked around, observing a flock of sheep coming down the slope. Strabo grabbed the reins of his horse and began walking up the hill to intercept them.

Both herdsmen were dressed in heavy coats made of sheepskin and wool and wore the Phrygian cap fashionable among the local male population.

"Greetings," Strabo said, right hand raised in a salute.

While the sheep continued their descent, the herdsmen stopped, resting with their hands and chin propped up on their long canes.

"Is this the way to Sarmizegetusa Regia?" Strabo said.

"Mhm," came the answer.

It seems they aren't the talkative kind.

"Do you speak Latin?" Strabo was not about to give up yet.

Wide grins greeted his question.

"I take that as a no." He shook his head, trying to figure out a way to communicate. "I assume you wouldn't know anything about the soldier murdered in the ruins up there."

The sheep brothers glanced at each other before caressing the talismans hanging from their necks. They wore the same symbol as Strabo's mother.

"No murder," one of them eventually said.

"What do—"

"No murder," the sheep brothers said in unison. "Go back! Go back!" With that said, they passed by Strabo and followed their flock down the slope.

******

The going was slow for most of the day because the slope was too steep, so Strabo had to lead his horse instead of riding it. He reached the top by late afternoon, and a vast grassy plateau opened before him. Strabo mounted and managed to cover half a dozen miles before the sun eventually dipped behind the mountains, and darkness slowly enveloped the land.

Strabo made camp next to a stream. He gathered some wood, lit a fire, and then used his canteen to prepare the legionary gruel he was so accustomed to by now. His dinner was enjoyable, though, thanks to the fresh bread, seasonings, cheese, and sausages his mother packed for the road.

Once sated, he rinsed clean his canteen in the cold waters of the stream. Finally, he poured some wine into his tin cup and heated it over the fire. The nights were still freezing up the mountains despite the coming of spring, so he could use the extra warmth provided by mulled wine.

He wrapped himself into the heavy wool blanket and propped his back against a large stone. The sky was clear, myriads of stars shining on the pitch-black background—it was breathtaking. On a night like this, one felt much closer to the gods. The stars, the crackling of the fire, the murmur of the water, and the occasional hooting of a night bird created an atmosphere filled with a kind of mystical tension.

Strabo tried to keep his mind focused on the mystery of the dead auxilia. Why did his mother suggest this might not be murder? Also, the herdsmen were adamant this wasn't a murder. Was it a suicide, then?

Highly unlikely; I never heard of anybody spearing himself to death.

There were more straightforward ways to commit suicide, especially for a Roman auxiliary soldier armed to the teeth.

On a different note, what was all the creepy talisman-caressing about? Strabo remembered his mother wearing the Dacian symbol since he was a small child. It was a kind of strange cross, with an inscribed circle in the middle and four curvy lines jutting out of it in all four directions.

Many years ago, Strabo asked his mother why she was wearing it. She said that it was a reminder of her Dacian heritage. Now he regretted not inquiring further about its meaning and symbolism.

Perhaps Hortensius was right, and it was a form of sacrifice. Although, as Strabo's father pointed out, Dacians were not known for practicing human sacrifice.

What if the attacker wasn't human? Was it why the locals claimed it wasn't a murder? Strabo chuckled, mentally mocking himself.

Lucius, you are going crazy!

Still, he recalled his mother's words, '*There is more to these woods than you might think.*' Despite his pragmatic worldview, a cold chill ran down his spine.

"Aaaaaauuuuuuuu!" Strabo jumped at the sounds of a distant howl.

"Aaaaaauuuuu!" By now, Strabo's worldly detachment was gone, and the icy hands of fear grabbed his soul as he added more logs to the fire. Was the source of the sound getting closer to him? Or was he imagining things?

Where did I put my sword?

He cursed.

******

It was a long and terrifying night. Strabo barely managed to get a couple of hours of sleep, his hand never leaving the legionary *gladius*' hilt. His imagination ran wild whenever he heard a ruffling of leaves or cracking of the trees' branches—he kept thinking about the horrors lurking in the woods around him.

With dawn and sunlight, reason reasserted itself.

Strabo felt ashamed now of his overreaction, especially since he had spent much of his childhood camping in these forests—it wasn't the first time he heard howling wolves. He glanced at his horse, addressing him in a severe tone. "Horsey, you are never to speak of this to anyone, understand?" Horsey snorted in derision.

Et tu, Brute?

III. Boys with Swords

Strabo reached the modest auxiliary fort by the early evening—he could see its shape against the dusky sky. As he approached it on horseback, the fires from its towers projected the shadows of sentries patrolling the timber walls.

"Who goes there?" came the eventual challenge.

"A friend," Strabo said.

"Approach, friend, and let me see you." Strabo rode in front of the gates, where the torches made him visible.

"I am *Frumentarius* Lucius Lucretius Strabo. Camp Praefect Hilarius of the *Gemina* sent me to investigate the death of your colleague."

"Wait there!"

After several moments the large oak gate opened with a loud creak. A man in a centurion's uniform stood on the other side, flanked by two auxiliaries.

"That was fast," the Centurion said. "I expected your arrival at least two days from now."

The officer was a middle-aged man. His double chin and round face testified to a cushy job guarding some ruins in the middle of nowhere.

"What can I say? I am a good rider," Strabo said as he dismounted and led his horse inside the fort.

The Centurion grunted. "I bet you are. So what does Praefect Hilarius want? We take our orders from Praefect Titianus, who in turn reports to the Legate of the Thirteenth."

Strabo stood at attention and raised his hand in the customary military salute. "*Frumentarius* Lucius Lucretius Strabo, reporting for duty. Hilarius is heading the local *frumentarii*. As of now, this investigation is an Imperial security matter."

"The Imperial secret service wants to investigate the murder of a non-citizen auxilia? Isn't Hilarius a bit paranoid?"

"Would you ask him directly, or should I convey your question, sir?"

The Centurion sighed deeply, and the fight went out of him.

"Very well, *Frumentarie*," he said, returning the salute. "Centurion Pacatus, commander of the Sixth Century of the First Pannonian Auxiliary Cohort. Our unit was detached to guard the ruins of Sarmizegetusa Regia."

Given the Centurion's out-of-shape appearance, Strabo was not surprised by his rank and the designation of his unit. Traditionally, the sixth consisted of trainees and raw recruits, meaning it was the least effective century of any cohort.

"Follow me!" Pacatus gestured. He led Strabo to his office in the main building. "You are hungry and tired, I presume."

"Yes, sir," Strabo said.

"Good, there isn't much I can tell you anyway." He sighed. "*Pedes* Blaesus' corpse was found by one of the patrols in the morning four days ago. Three spears pierced his chest, belly, and throat. The patrol brought the body here, and our medic confirmed the cause of death."

Pedes, Strabo noted. *Blaesus was a footman, a simple private.*

"Can I see the body?"

"No, can't do. We incinerated him yesterday."

Fuck, this will make things harder.

"Blaesus? That's a Dacian name, right?

Pacatus shook his head. "How should I know? All these barbarian names sound the same to me."

Although Roman auxiliary troops were recruited from the non-citizen *peregrini*, the free provincial subjects of the Empire, traditionally, the centurions were Roman citizens of Italian descent. Thankfully, having the first African emperor on the throne wasn't an outlier but part of a broader trend of provincial citizens gradually replacing the Italian gentry from leadership positions. The Centurion's appearance and behavior did nothing to challenge the necessity of the power shift—on the contrary.

In the face of Pacatus' snobbery, Strabo maintained his professional demeanor. He rephrased the question and said, "Where was he from?"

"*Thracia*, I believe. Somewhere just south of the *Danubius* river."

Strabo's mother warned him that if the victim was from *Dacia*, *Thracia*, or *Moesia*, it might not be a murder.

"I assume most of your men are young recruits."

"Just off their mothers' tits." Pacatus spat.

"How many of them are Thracians?"

"Most are from *Pannonia*. Only two dozen or so are Thracians, so I grouped them into three *contubernia*. They seem not to enjoy the company of others."

"Any suspects?"

"No one specifically but the Thracians didn't get along with the Pannonians. I would start there if I were you."

"I see, so you haven't done any investigation since?"

"Of course I did." Pacatus bristled. "Who do you think I am? Some brainless recruit?" Strabo decided it would be better to refrain from sharing his opinion on the matter.

Pacatus continued, "I have interrogated his tent, and nobody seems to know anything."

"Shocking," Strabo muttered under his breath.

Pacatus snapped. "What's that?"

"I was wondering what he was doing at the ruins."

"I have no clue; he wasn't supposed to be there. Instead, he should have been sleeping in his tent. His *decanus* and tent-mates swore Blaesus was there when they went to sleep. But, he was missing at the morning inspection, so I suspect he sneaked out during the night."

"Anybody saw him leave the fort?"

"No, the sentries haven't seen anybody leaving."

"Still, he obviously left somehow."

"Obviously," Pacatus said dryly.

"Could the sentries be lying?"

"It is more likely they were sleeping; I had all sixteen of them publicly flogged, just in case. It's too bad decimation is not an acceptable punishment in these peaceful days."

"Yeah, too bad."

In the past, legionaries and auxiliaries who fell asleep on sentry duty were ritually beaten to death by their tent-mates to remind the others not to endanger the unit by slacking. This form of punishment was called a *decimation,* even if it didn't necessarily imply killing every tenth man from a unit.

"Look, *Frumentarie*, we are both tired, so you should go and rest. We have comfortable officers' baths—I will have dinner brought to your room by the time you finish. Then, in the morning, you can interrogate whoever you want, alright?"

"Thank you, sir. I appreciate your cooperation."

******

The baths were as comfy as Pacatus said. There were no fancy frescos or marble floors, but the installations functioned efficiently. Strabo lounged in the hot pool, soaking his aching body in the soothing water. It was an excellent time to go over the case.

A Thracian recruit named Blaesus was found dead among the ruins of Sarmizegetusa Regia four mornings ago—three spears pierced his body. Strabo decided to pause here for a bit.

Upon hearing about the spears, his mother, a Dacian by birth, immediately suspected the victim might be either a local or hailed from the neighboring provinces.

What do these people have in common?

Strabo wasn't very knowledgeable about the history of the barbarians, despite his mother's origins. However, he served in the Thirteenth Legion with countless soldiers from these provinces. Although they were Roman citizens by birth, many legionaries were of local descent. Their fathers received citizenship at the end of their 26-year-long military service in the Roman auxiliary units.

He recalled the Dacian, Thracian, and Moesian soldiers spoke to each other in the local dialect when off duty—they had no issues communicating even though they originated from different provinces. Furthermore, some wore the same symbol as his mother and the herdsmen Strabo encountered earlier. Given all these elements, it was safe to assume these tribes were related and worshiped the same gods.

What about the death-by-spears part?

It was most probably connected to the religion shared by the locals, but Strabo had no clue how. All he knew was the spears indicated Blaesus was not the victim of a murder—at least, according to the locals he had talked to so far.

But what else could it be if not murder?

Some sort of ceremonial suicide was doubtful for practical reasons—it was hard to spear oneself, especially three times, once through the belly, once through the chest, and once through the throat. Blaesus would have probably died after receiving the first wound, whichever it was. Even if that wouldn't have killed him, the second one would definitely have. Thus, he couldn't use the third spear. *Ergo*, this was not suicide.

Human sacrifice, voluntary or otherwise, seemed equally unlikely. First, none of the local or neighboring people were known to practice human sacrifice, now or in the past. Second, the garrison's surgeon confirmed that the spear wounds were the cause of death. Lastly, if it had been the case, Pacatus would have surely mentioned ritual disemboweling or other forms of mutilation associated with religious sacrifice.

So what else could it be, if not murder, suicide, or sacrifice? And how was this related to the local religion?

For now, Strabo decided to drop this line of inquiry and focus on how Blaesus got to the ruins.

A *contubernium*, or tent, was the basic military unit, both in the legions and the auxiliary cohorts. It consisted of a ten men squad sharing an actual tent—eight fighting men, including the *decanus*, plus a couple of non-combatant servants.

According to his tent mates, the victim was in bed when they all got to sleep that night. Based on his own legionary experience, Strabo couldn't imagine how Blaesus could have stumbled out of a pitch-dark tent without waking up at least one of his sleeping mates. The only logical conclusion was that the tent mates lied. *But why would they?*

A loud growl of his stomach reminded Strabo that he hadn't eaten since morning. Therefore, he decided to get out of the water and scrub himself while still possessing the necessary energy.

IV. A Deadly Interview

Strabo woke up to the sounds of the morning inspection. Very. Early. Morning.

He dressed up as fast as he could, washed his face, and arranged his ruffled hair before leaving his room.

The whole century of fighting men—79 auxiliary soldiers now that Blaesus was dead—assembled in orderly rows. At a glance, one could hardly tell the difference between a legionary unit and its auxiliary infantry counterpart—the men wore similar helmets and armor and used the same *gladius* sword and *pugio* dagger. The main visible difference was the shield; while the legionary *scutum* was rectangular, the auxiliary was oval.

For a trained eye, though, there were other tell-tale signs. For example, some of the assembled auxiliaries had bows on their backs instead of the standard legionary throwing spear, the *pilum*. Also, the rows of men standing at attention were almost imperceptibly crooked, a testament to a lower quality of training and discipline.

Centurion Pacatus reviewed his troops, the vine cane symbolizing his rank in hand. As any centurion was expected to do, he shouted invectives while using cane blows to emphasize his points. One hapless auxiliary failed to polish his body armor to Pacatus's otherwise low standards, so he was rewarded with a heavy blow on his Gallic helmet. *Ouch, that must have hurt—a lot.*

The garrison commander finished walking down the rows and returned to the front to address the century.

"Men, let me introduce our guest." Pacatus gestured for Strabo to join him. "This is *Frumentarius* Strabo. In his infinite wisdom, the commander of the *frumentarii* decided to send him to shed light on Footman Blaesus' untimely death. You are to cooperate with Lucretius Strabo and answer all his questions. The sooner this issue is resolved, the sooner our guest will leave, allowing us to return to our lovely routine. Is this understood?"

"Yes, Centurion Pacatus, sir!"

"Good. You are dismissed!"

"You heard the Centurion; get on with your duties, you poor excuse of men," the Optio said, just in case Pacatus' wasn't clear enough. *Army life was such a joy.*

******

"Are you sure Blaesus was in the tent when you fell asleep?"

"Yes, sir."

"And you haven't seen him leaving?"

"No, sir."

"I see. How would you describe Footman Blaesus?"

"He was a good lad, a credit to our *contubernium* and the Sixth Century." Strabo already knew the answer by heart.

"Was he religious? What gods did he worship?"

"Not any god in particular. He was a… .what's the word…."

"Polytheist?"

"Yes, he was a polytheist, sir."

Strabo sighed deeply. He was interrogating the sixth man from the late Blaesus' tent. They all said the same thing, using precisely the same words—clearly, the answers were rehearsed.

"You are dismissed. Please send in the last one on your way out."

The seventh guy entered the room. His eye was bruised and swollen, and a bloody bandage covered his left shoulder.

"What happened to you?"

"Aaah, nothing, sir. I mean, it was an accident."

Strabo wasn't convinced. "You fell with your face into somebody's fist?"

"No, sir, the door hit me."

"I see. The door from your tent hit you?"

"Exactly, sir…I mean, no, tents have no doors."

"Indeed, they don't."

The man began to fidget under his interrogator's steady gaze.

It must be the eyepatch. It makes me look ferocious.

Strabo pushed on. "What about the bandage?"

The soldier was sweating by now. Something was definitely fishy.

"What is your name, *Pedes*?"

"Cotiso, sir."

Strabo stood up and approached within inches of his victim's face. "Look, Cotiso, I am not your commander. I couldn't care less if you fought with one of your buddies. But I don't particularly appreciate being lied to. As a *frumentarius*, I could have you tortured just for fun. Is this what you want?"

Cotiso gulped before squeaking, "N-n-no, sir."

"Good, me neither—the screams and blood make me lose my appetite." Strabo threw Cotiso a meaningful look to reinforce his point before returning behind Pacatus's desk. "Let's try this again. I ask a question, and then you answer it. Truthfully! How about that?"

Cotiso nodded hesitantly.

"Judging by the color of your eye, you took a beating a few days ago. When exactly?"

"Five days ago, sir."

"I assume it happened during the evening, somewhere out of sight. Otherwise, the *optio*, the *tesserarius*, or one of the *decani* would intervene. Is this correct?"

"Yes, sir."

"It happened during the same night Blaesus died, right?"

Silence. Cotiso trembled like a leaf by now. *He is scared shitless.*

"Do you know what happened to Blaesus?"

The guy was close to breaking point, and it was time to push him harder. Strabo slammed both his hands on the wooden table. "Tell me what happened, or I'll beat it out of you, one word at a time!"

Suddenly the door opened, and Pacatus's second in command, *Optio* Dardanos, entered. "Excuse my interruption, *Frumentarie*, but Centurion Pacatus wants to see you."

"Now? I am in the middle of something." The interruption vexed Strabo.

"I am afraid it can't wait." *Fucking Pacatus, I was this close to breaking Cotiso.*

"You stay right here." Strabo pointed at Cotiso. "We will continue our little chat when I am back."

He stormed out of the office, searching for Pacatus. The commander was nowhere to be seen on the large parade ground. *Where the hell is he?* Strabo walked to the mess hall, suspecting the Centurion dropped by for a quick snack. Nothing. "Fuck him," he said out loud.

Strabo retraced his steps planning to resume Cotiso's interrogation. He entered the main administrative building, the *principia*, turned left on the corridor, and opened Pacatus' office door.

"Oh no." He couldn't believe his eye. "This can't be happening!" Strabo tried to control the anger swelling inside him—unsuccessfully. "I was out only for a few fucking moments!" Strabo shouted at Cotiso's limply swinging body.

The man was dead, hanged with his leather belt by one of the room's wooden beams.

******

"He's dead alright," the *capsarius* nodded. Strabo and Pacatus exchanged a sour look.

"Thank you, *Capsarie*. I can't imagine where we'd be without your expert support."

The middle-aged paramedic shrugged, the sarcasm bouncing off him.

Strabo clenched his fists in frustration. "He was hiding something, of that I am sure. I was close to breaking him when your man, Dardanos, called me away."

"I see." Pacatus nodded, then shrugged, seemingly unconcerned by the developments. "Well, I assume your mission here is over. At least we can take comfort in that."

Strabo was incredulous. "What do you mean?"

Pacatus sighed, a self-satisfied smile blooming on his fat face. "Isn't it obvious? Cotiso killed Blaesus. When he realized you were onto him, he took his own life rather than face the torturers. Case closed!"

Strabo was tempted to wipe away the Centurion's stupid smile with a punch or two, but he said instead, "I believe you are wrong…sir."

"Why else would he hang himself?"

"I think the question isn't *why,* but *how* did he hang himself." Strabo gestured at the scene. "Look, the beam is pretty high up. He couldn't have reached it."

"Come now, Strabo. He climbed on one of the chairs, obviously."

"But there is no chair under him, and the nearest one is several feet away."

Strabo's observation confused Pacatus. "Well…I…he…but…"

"My thoughts exactly," Strabo said once it became apparent that Pacatus's vocabulary ran out of one-syllable words.

"Somebody must have helped him," the *capsarius* butted in.

Strabo opened his arms, admiring the paramedic's mental acuity. "Right on point, *amice.* At least one of us is paying attention." Pacatus' usually purple face turned red, but he had the common sense to swallow any witty retort that might have crossed his mind.

Strabo continued his explanation, "Dardanos was the only one in the room when I left, and the other six men from Cotiso's unit were outside. Which leads to an important question: why did you call me away? It was perfect timing, so to speak."

"W-w-what are you talking about? I didn't call you anywhere."

Fatty is not smiling anymore.

"Dardanos interrupted my interrogation of Cotiso, saying you want to see me urgently."

"Well, he was lying. I didn't."

"Where were you during my interrogation sessions, sir?"

"I…I…I was…I was…" He gave up with a loud sigh and gestured at the field medic. "Tardus, please share my whereabouts with *Frumentarius* Strabo."

The *capsarius* seemed amused by the problematic situation his commander was in. "Are you sure, Centurion? Our guest might not approve…."

"Just tell him!" Pacatus snapped.

"Yes, sir, at once, sir!" Tardus turned toward Strabo, standing at attention. "*Frumentarie* Strabo, sir. Allow me to report that Centurion Pacatus was in the sick bay the whole morning. I can assure you he had no contact with Dardanos or any other member of the garrison during this time, sir."

"How can you be so sure?" Strabo said.

A huge grin split Tardus' face as he said, "Because he was sleeping, sir."

"He was doing what?"

"He was sleeping in one of the medical beds, sir." The *capsarius* continued his report with a straight face, "You know, sir, the burdens of command can weigh down a man, even one as strong as Centurion Pacatus."

Tardus might be slow, but once he catches on…

Judging by the expression on his face, Pacatus could have murdered the field medic on the spot if not for the presence of an Imperial agent.

"If you haven't called me then….Fuck!" Realization dawned upon Strabo. "Where is Cotiso's tent? Quick, let's go!"

They hurried out of the main building and toward the sleeping quarters of the auxiliaries. Pacatus led the way between the rows of tents. Eventually, he stopped in front of one, opened the flap, and stepped inside. The tent was empty.

"Where could they be at this hour of the day?"

"I specifically ordered the Thracians not to leave the fort, given your investigation and all. Let's check at the gate."

A couple of guards stood at attention as they saw their commander approaching the main exit. "Have you seen Dardanos passing by?" an out-of-breath Pacatus said.

"Yes, sir. *Optio* Dardanos and three *contubernia* left a while ago."

"Three *contubernia*? Which ones?"

"The Thracians, sir. The *Optio* took them out for a drill."

Pacatus turned toward Strabo; desperation was written all over his face. They stared at each other, not knowing what to say.

Eventually, *Capsarius* Tardus broke the silence, "I think I know who helped Cotiso hang himself."

As I said, there is no stopping him once he catches on.

V. The Good Old Doctor

"Let's go over this again," Centurion Pacatus suggested. They were in the commander's office, the entire garrison on high alert by now.

Strabo nodded and explained, "Footman Blaesus was found speared to death in the ruins of Sarmizegetusa Regia. Five days later, one of his tent-mates was hanged during a break into his interrogation. Lastly, your deputy and all of the Thracian auxiliaries left the fort without permission."

Pacatus paced around the room. "Where does this leave us, Strabo?"

"It leaves us with many questions." Strabo shook his head. "First, how did Blaesus exit the tent on that ominous night without waking up any of his mates?"

"Most likely, he did wake them. So they knew he left."

"What about the gates? How could he sneak out?"

Pacatus smiled sadly, then said, "The other two Thracian *contubernia* were on guard duty that night."

"They probably let Blaesus out, then. Still, did he leave alone, or did others from his unit join him?"

"I don't know." Pacatus grew more despondent.

"Me neither. Let's move on to the next set of questions." Strabo scratched his chin and continued, "When I pushed Cotiso, he seemed ready to break. At that moment, *Optio* Dardanos, presumably eavesdropping on the other side of the door, barged in and interrupted me. He made sure I left the scene so they could murder Cotiso before he could spill their secret—whatever that might be."

"Sounds about right," Pacatus said.

"Realising that we will eventually figure out this was not a suicide, Dardanos and all his accomplices, the auxiliaries from Thracia, deserted their posts."

"Yes, yes. But why did they murder Blaesus in the first place?"

Strabo tut-tutted at the Centurion's habit of stating the obvious. He said, "That is the million *sesterces* question, isn't it?"

"Well, you are the *frumentarius*. Find out what happened." Pacatus' voice was mildly hysterical, and he had difficulty controlling his nerves. No wonder he was the commander of the sixth century of an auxiliary cohort—he could never have made it to legionary centurion.

"Hmm, something was strange about Cotiso. I mean, even before he ended up hanging from the ceiling."

Pacatus stared at him expectantly, his eyebrows raised in a question.

Strabo said, "All the other Thracians stonewalled me; shamelessly and confidently. But Cotiso was trembling, ready to break."

"He might have been weaker than the others."

"Well, was he? You were his commander, after all."

"Not that I recall. He seemed like a strong, reliable lad." Pacatus sighted. "Then again, all the Thracian boys seemed to be strong, reliable lads."

Strabo stood up. "I need to talk to the *capsarius*. Cotiso was beaten up the night Blaesus died, and maybe our good-old sawbones noticed something out of the ordinary."

"I wouldn't count on it." Pacatus grinned. "Tardus is not exactly the sharpest blade of the century, if you know what I mean."

"He seemed sharp enough to me." Strabo was almost out the door when Pacatus called after him.

"Strabo, what about the deserters?"

"What about them?"

"Should I send soldiers to apprehend them?"

I love decisive commanders.

"I wouldn't if I were you. They had no compunction about murdering one of their own in the middle of a military fort—what is to stop them from ambushing the patrols? I suggest you send a courier to Praefect Hilarius requesting a couple of centuries as reinforcements."

The Centurion bristled. "Aren't you exaggerating a bit? Deserters are usually crucified, so Dardanos and the others are probably a dozen miles away already."

"Perhaps you are right. But I have a very bad feeling about this entire situation."

******

The sickbay was in a timber building similar to the one housing Pacatus's office. The entrance opened to a large room with four empty beds on each side; ceiling-to-floor curtains separated the back section.

Strabo peeked behind the curtains. He noticed a wooden table in the center and different medical instruments placed on pegs and wall shelves—it must have been the surgery room. There were two other tables on the left side, one empty, the other containing a covered body, most probably Cotiso's.

He turned away from the curtains.

Strabo guessed that the door on the right wall led to Tardus' private lodgings. He knocked.

"Tardus, are you there?"

"I am coming." Strabo could hear Tardus' mumblings. "Can't a man have some peace in this godsforsaken place?"

The door opened, revealing the half-asleep paramedic.

"How can you sleep when the fort is on high alert?"

"Well," the *capsarius* said while scratching his head, "unless somebody is hurt, I am not of too much use. Better to get out of the way."

"Mhm. Anyway, I want to ask you some questions about Cotiso."

"Go ahead, sir." Tardus gestured for Strabo to sit down on one of the beds.

"Footman Cotiso had a swollen eye, and his upper body was bandaged. Was it your handiwork?"

"Yes, sir. He dropped in at dawn several days ago."

"The same morning Blaesus' body was found in the Dacian ruins?"

Tardus needed a few heartbeats to search the dusty library that was his memory. Eventually, he found what he was looking for.

"Indeed, sir, the same morning. I remember because we had red beans for breakfast. I love red beans, served with fresh bread, fried chicken egg, and onions." Tardus swallowed at the thought of his favorite food. "I love onions too…"

"Focus, man!"

The paramedic looked down at his sandals avoiding eye contact. "Sorry, sir. Where was I?"

Strabo forced himself to be calm. He had nothing to gain by shouting at Speedy here. "You were telling me about the early morning Cotiso required medical attention."

"Oh, yes. As I said, he dropped in the door. I was in my room, washing my face, when I heard him crash on the wooden floor. His tunic was soaked, blood squirting from a piercing wound on his chest. Fortunately, it was only superficial despite the heavy bleeding—I managed to stop it and stitch the wound."

"What kind of weapon could leave those wounds?" Strabo whispered, careful not to interrupt Tardus' delicate thought processes.

"I don't think it was a *gladius* because the wound was not wide enough."

"I understand; it wasn't a *gladius*. What else could it have been?"

Tardus was so deep in thought that he forgot himself and began scratching his balls methodically. "It couldn't be a *pugio* either. The wound was not deep enough, you see."

Strabo exploded. "So what the hell was it?"

The *capsarius* blinked a couple of times expressionlessly, and his eyes glazed, out of focus. Then the blinking restarted. *That's it; I fried his brain.*

Strabo leaned closer to Tardus' face, looking directly into his victim's unrestrained eyes. He lifted his index finger and moved it left and right in front of the paramedic's face. *Nothing.* He snapped his fingers, trying to get a reaction—still nothing.

"Jupiter Optimus Maximus, what have I done?" Strabo said out loud.

He grabbed Tardus' shoulders with both hands and gently shook him. "Come on, man. Snap out of it!" He shook him more violently, but still no response. "Come on," Strabo said, punching Tardus with his right fist out of frustration.

Brrrrrrrrr! A loud noise came out from Tardus' backside. Brrrrrrrrrrrr! Strabo backed off in a panic, concerned about the reaction he had provoked.

"Sorry, sir. Must have been the red beans." The blinking stopped, and Tardus was once again in the here and now as if nothing had happened. "Where was I? Oh yes, I think Cotiso was wounded with a spear of some kind. Let me show you." With that said, the paramedic walked behind the curtain to the surgery room.

Strabo was too shocked to speak, unable to comprehend what had just happened. *What the fuck is wrong with this guy?*

Regaining his wits, he followed the field medic; he found him standing above the naked body of Cotiso.

"See? The wound is similar to the ones on Blaesus' body, but the spear hasn't penetrated very deep in Cotiso's case." He gestured for Strabo to lean closer and see for himself. Apart from the stitched wound on the left part of his chest, Strabo observed a couple of deep blue bruises, one on the right shoulder and the other on the left hip.

"What about these bruises?"

Tardus pointed to the bluish stains on Cotiso's otherwise white body, "You see the pattern? It is dark blue in the middle of each spot, and then it gets lighter on the edges."

Strabo nodded and then said, "What could create such a pattern?"

"Ah, that's easy." The *capsarius* smiled. "Spears also provoked these. However, the spearheads failed to penetrate the body and glanced off the hip and shoulder bones. So, it left these interesting bruising patterns."

Strabo couldn't believe his ears. "Are you telling me three spears wounded Cotiso just like Blaesus?"

"Yes, sir."

"On the very same night?"

"Precisely, sir."

"And...," *careful not to freeze him again,* "you knew this," *breath in, breath out,* "since five days ago?"

"Of course, sir. I am a *capsarius*, after all." Tardus puffed out his chest, proud of his mental acuity.

Strabo's face was red, and his head was ready to explode. But he worried about Tardus' fragile state, so he stopped himself from shouting. Instead, he hissed, "And you didn't think of informing Pacatus or me about this?"

The paramedic had an offended expression on his face. "You never asked, sir!"

"Thank you, Tardus," Strabo whispered before leaving the building, careful not to slam the door behind him.

It was already dark outside, so Strabo decided to retire for the night. He walked to the guest room located in the command building, undressed, and carefully washed his body using the sponge and the water bowl. Once clean, he dropped down on his bed, staring at the ceiling in a vain attempt to calm himself.

The soldiers on guard duty would never forget the sudden, blood-curdling cry that pierced the night. Nobody knew for certain what kind of monstrous creature could have roared like that, but some could swear the sound came from within the camp.

VI. In the Shadow of Kings

The following day Strabo decided to visit the ruins. Blaesus's body was found there, and Cotiso might have been wounded in the same place around the same time. Despite the risk of running into the deserters, Pacatus' protestations against this course of action were subdued—it seemed the centurion was not very fond of Strabo.

The ruins of the old Dacian capital were just a few miles away. Consequently, Strabo chose to walk instead of riding. He left the road linking the garrison to the Apulum—Ulpia Traiana Sarmizegetusa highway and continued on a footpath through the woods. The morning sun shone through the leaves, birdsong filling the crisp mountain air.

After an hour or so of steady walking, the woods opened up to a large clearing. The outlines of what was once a defensive stone wall were clearly visible. Strabo climbed over the ruined encirclement and took in the sights in front of him.

He could see the foundations of a couple of square buildings to his left, some sort of round stone altar in front of the closest square shape. *The building was probably a temple before Traianus' troops destroyed it.*

The timber stilts jutting out of the ground were a testament to a large, round edifice that once towered above the altar—it must have been a gathering place. It didn't take much intellectual effort on Strabo's behalf to conclude that he was looking at the remains of the ancient capital's sacred district.

Strabo walked to the altar. The rust-brown color of dry blood was faintly visible on the gray stone. *It must be where they found Blaesus' body.* It was almost a week ago, but the stains were still discernable, indicating that a lot of blood was spilled. *So Blaesus was not only found here but was stabbed on this very spot.*

He carefully looked around. The ground surrounding the altar was not perfectly even, so rainwater tended to form puddles. Since the last rain, the water dried up, but several sunbaked footprints were left on the ground. *Hmmm, that is interesting.* He kneeled and analyzed the soil using the pathfinding skills he learned as an intelligence operative of *Legio XIII Gemina.*

Strabo could easily distinguish the prints belonging to five different individuals, and the size of the feet suggested all of them were males. The depths and shapes of the tracks indicated that the people who left them were standing put. These were not the kind of prints left by walking. *Could they belong to the patrol which found Blaesus's body?*

"They could, then again…," Strabo said out loud. Something wasn't right. "Why would a handful of soldiers stand packed together, breathing down each others' necks?"

Based on his experience, people had a morbid curiosity when confronted with dead people. Strabo would have expected the shocked patrolmen to surround the victim and gawk.

However, there was ample space for the auxiliaries to do that without stepping off the round stony surface serving as an altar.

"Yet, some stood in rows, on the then-wet earth, facing the altar, as indicated by the footprints." Strabo could think of only one logical explanation. At that time, the space was packed, with no room to fan out. *Ergo*, these footprints didn't belong to the men who found the victim's body but to a significantly larger group.

Strabo stepped back to the center of the round stone, trying to estimate how many people could stand around its circumference. Its radius was circa three feet, which meant a rim of….of….*fuck it*! Strabo couldn't remember the formulas he learned in school.

He guestimated that 20 people could stand around the altar. The three Thracian tents comprised 24 auxiliaries plus six servants. For the gathered to stay packed in several rows, as the footprints indicated, there must have been at least thrice that number. *But who were the others?*

He went back to the tracks, this time inspecting them more carefully. Now that he knew what to look for, he realized that some impressions were made by military hobnailed sandals while others by plain-soled footwear. "Civilians? In the middle of nowhere, miles away from any settlement?" *That was strange.*

It seemed that a large group of people, probably 60 or more, composed of soldiers and civilians, gathered here for some kind of ritual—based on the evidence, this was a high probability deduction. Strabo was satisfied with his findings, although he couldn't guess the identity of the civilians. Now he had to establish the *when* part.

Since he arrived two nights ago, there has been no rain. Also, the day he rode, the earth was dry, so probably there was no rain the day before that either. The last time it could have rained was four days ago, while Blaesus was found six mornings ago.

He focused on the bloodstain. The rusty brown spatter was still visible almost a week later. If it had been rained, the stain would have been washed away already, or at least it would have been smudged.

Lastly, the fort was in lockdown since the morning Blaesus was found, and the only auxiliaries who left the garrison's fort were the deserters, but that was only yesterday. Even if Dardanos' men had come here yesterday with two dozen civilians in tow, the earth was already dry enough to prevent these kinds of deep imprints.

There was no recent rainfall, no smudging of the bloodstains left by the victim, and no other Roman soldiers who could have visited after Blaesus's death. Hence, it seemed safe to assume that the large gathering and Blaesus' untimely demise happened around the same time.

Strabo closed his eyes, trying to imagine the scene. It was the middle of the night, flaming torches lighting up the faces of the dozens of people packed around the stone altar, Dardanus and the Thracian auxiliaries among them. The mob watched as auxiliary Blaesus bled out, three spears jutting out of his body.

If this wasn't human sacrifice, what the hell could it have been?

******

The sun soon reached its zenith, slowly descending toward the west. It was unseasonably warm for Dacia in early spring, and Strabo sweated profusely. Content with the fact that there were no other clues left around the altar, he moved to inspect the ruins of what could have been a large gathering hall.

"Ptiuuu." He whistled in admiration. "The size of the building must have been impressive, by barbarian standards, that is."

"Halt!" The voice boomed as Strabo prepared to step into the circle of the remaining stilts. His heart stopped for a moment at the sudden noise. Then, before he could regain his composure and glance at its source, the demanding voice continued, " Who dares disturb the sacred temple of Zalmoxis?"

Finally, Strabo managed to turn and saw an older man angrily pointing at him with his oaken staff. He was just a few feet away. The man's gray hair flowed down his shoulders, his long gray beard trimmed and tied through a golden ring. His eyes were red with fury.

"Well, this 'Moxis guy of yours should take better care of his temple." Strabo pointed to the ruins.

Apparently, Graybeard lacked a sense of humor, for he raised his staff and aimed a sundering blow at Strabo's head. Strabo's quick reflexes allowed him to step out of the way, barely avoiding a potentially fatal wound. Instead, the staff hit the ground leaving the crazy old man in a precarious balance—Strabo pushed him just enough for Graybeard to land on his back and drop his makeshift weapon.

"Careful, now, you wouldn't want to hurt one of the Emperor's finest." Strabo kicked the staff out of his aggressor's reach. Graybeard's face turned pale as he slowly got up, his anger and frustration boiling.

Now that the imminent danger was gone, Strabo could size up the man. He wore a once-white tunic, the familiar Dacian symbol embroidered on his chest.

"Are you a priest?" Strabo said. "I know that symbol; my mother always wears it."

Graybeard spat at Strabo's feet.

"What are you doing here? This site is off-limits by order of the Emperor."

Hearing this, Graybeard's look of utter hatred got even more profound. He hissed, "Your Emperor means nothing to me."

"We'll see about that once you meet our lovely torturers. You are under arrest on suspicion of murdering Footman Blaesus on this very spot."

Graybeard smiled as his gaze slid beyond Strabo's shoulders. "I don't think so."

Strabo turned to see a large group of armed men approaching, some of them wearing the scarlet tunics of the auxiliary cohorts. He immediately realized he couldn't fight them off, and running was the only option. So, he whirled by the now-grinning priest as he made his way toward the nearest trees.

"Bring the Roman to me!" Graybeard's shouted orders followed the departing Strabo.

He ran as he never did before, up the wooded hill, careful not to bang into a tree or stumble on the rocky ground. The climb got steeper, and he had to drop on all fours as he continued his desperate flight. His pursuers closed in on him; Strabo could hear their calls and jeers but forced himself not to glance back and focus on the path ahead. His face was torn as he pushed on through the bushes.

He couldn't see much ahead but must have been close to the top because the incline became less abrupt. Strabo had to crawl because the vegetation between the trees was too thick for him to stand or even kneel. He pushed on and on, and then…there was no more ground below him. He fell from the cliff's edge, hitting the ground and then uncontrollably rolling down the slope.

The last thing he heard was a loud thud as his head banged into something hard. Everything went dark.

VII. The Goddess of the Hunt

His world was enveloped in darkness. He tried to open his eye, but a sharp pain overwhelmed him. "Mmmm," he heard himself moaning.

Something cold and wet touched the back of his head, soothing his pain. This time, Strabo lifted his eyelid just enough to see a beautiful woman looking back. Her blond hair flowed over her heart-shaped face as she leaned above him, a hand under his head, holding a damp cloth against the swallowing bump.

"Hush now," she said softly. "You'll be fine." She smiled a mesmerizingly white smile, and her deep green eyes blinked reassuringly as if in a nod. Strabo realized the lady had a hunting bow on her back. *A beautiful huntress*, he thought.

He tried to talk, but his throat was too dry. His savior held a wooden cup to his lips, a bitter liquid pouring into his mouth.

"No, no, drink this. It is good for you, " she said when he tried to move his head away.

"Diana…"

"Rest now," she cooed.

******

The smell of food woke him. He squinted and stared into a starlit sky—Strabo was on his back, facing upwards. Judging by the moon's position, he deduced that the sun had set a couple of hours ago.

Strabo tilted his head toward the sound of crackling firewood. The goddess from his dreams was busy cooking something in a metallic pot. The smell was delicious.

"Diana?" he whispered.

She looked up from the pot and smiled. "Feeling better?"

"W-w-w….who are you?"

Before approaching Strabo, she scooped some of the pot's content into a wooden bowl. Then, she helped Strabo sit up and lean against a tree stump.

"Let's see your head. Please don't move."

Strabo realized his upper head was covered in a makeshift bandage. The lady carefully removed the cloth and inspected the wound on the back of his head.

"Hmm, the swelling subsided quite rapidly. That's good." She poured clean water on the cloth from her canteen before bandaging Strabo's head again. As she finished, the woman returned to Strabo's visual range, picked up the bowl, and offered it to him. "Eat this, slowly, and then rest. Come the morning, and you'll be well enough to travel."

Strabo took the vessel—it contained a brown-yellow soup, the leg of a fowl, mushrooms, and wild thyme. He sampled the liquid and was surprised to experience the sweet taste of his mother's cooking.

She joined him, eating directly from the pot. They dined in silence. Once they finished, the woman offered her canteen.

"I'll go wash these." She gathered the bowl, the pot, and the spoon and left Strabo's visual range once more.

Although his head throbbed in pain, he felt better with his belly full. He carefully leaned down on his back, trying to find a comfortable position for his wounded head.

Who was his savior? Could she really be the goddess Diana?

He waited for her return, determined not to let her off the hook this time. His curiosity, though, wasn't enough to keep him awake—he fell asleep.

******

"Rise and shine." She prodded gently.

Strabo stared into the face of the goddess, the morning light hallowing her. "Diana?"

She rolled her eyes in mock jealousy. "No, it is just me, the humble wench who saved your life." The dumb look on his face must have discouraged further cheeky comments. "How do you feel?"

He moved his head, cautiously probing for pain. "I think I am ok, in a shitty *I-wish-I-was-dead* kind of way."

"Aren't we all?" She stood up. "Come now, have a bite. We have a long journey ahead of us."

"Err....we do?"

She scoffed. "What would Diana think of me if I left you bumbling aimlessly in the woods?"

Strabo was confused. "Which Diana?"

"I was wondering the same thing. So let's start with the beginning, ok? Who are you, and how did you land in my woods?"

The previous day's events flashed before his eyes—the clues pointing to Blaesus' ritual murder, the crazed old man, and the mob howling for Strabo's blood.

"I am Lucius Lucretius Strabo, a *frumentarius* attached to the Thirteenth. I was investigating the Dacian ruins when a mob attacked me. I must have fallen off a cliff during the chase."

"A *frumentarius*, eh? I expected more from the Emperor's finest." She grinned.

"I tend to have this effect on women. Now, care to fill me in on the rest?"

"I am Dochia; I live in a nearby village. I was tracking deer when I stumbled into you. You are not exactly the game I was looking for."

"Thank you for tending to my wounds, Dochia."

"I have a weak spot for helpless puppies." She pointed behind him. "There is a stream there. Wash your face, let's eat, and move on. I will walk you to a village to the south, and you can rest there until you are able to travel to Apulum."

He stood up on shaky legs. Strabo had to lean on a boulder to steady the whirling world.

"I need to go to the small fort near Sarmizegetusa Regia. That should be to the north of here."

Dochia looked away in embarrassment. "The mob that chased you, who were they?"

"A bunch of deserters joined by a score of locals. A priestly-looking bloke led them."

"Long gray hair and beard, right?"

Strabo scrutinized her suspiciously. "Who is he?"

She shrugged. "A deluded old man, clinging to a long gone past. We should go as far away from him as possible. And that's why we will go south."

He stared at her for a long time, trying to decide his next move. Dochia was right; going north would increase the risk of bumping into those lunatics. However, moving southward and then traveling to Apulum on the highway might take a couple of days, assuming he was fit to ride a horse from one of the legionary courier stables.

"Can you be a bit more specific?" Strabo said.

Dochia flashed a mischievous smile. "You first. Who is Diana?"

Strabo blushed in embarrassment, recalling how he mistook her for the goddess of the hunt. *I mean, she is sexy and has a bow, right? No dog, tough…*

"Well…you see…I mistook you for someone else, that's all."

"Can you be a bit more specific?" she said, mirroring his earlier question.

"Err…there is this lady, you know, a huntress, and she looks a bit like you." She must have noticed his burning ears, for she pushed on shamelessly. "And is this lady a friend of yours?"

"Not exactly; I mean, I hope she is. I did sacri….err…offered her gifts now and then…."

"Oh no? You thought I was the goddess Diana! No, no….that is alright…no need to feel embarrassed. Tell me more, please."

He walked toward the stream, hoping it was deep enough to drown out her incessant laughter.

VIII. The Name of the Enemy

It turned out that Graybeard's real name was Decaeneus, and he claimed to be the high priest of Zalmoxis, the now-forgotten deity of the Dacians. Dochia saw him during her childhood, roaming the villages and agitating for rebellion against the Romans. Then, one day he suddenly disappeared, and everybody assumed the authorities had arrested him. Whatever the case, he was back with a vengeance.

"You are not listening, Strabo! Decaeneus gathered a large following this time, and the bloodletting is imminent. Dacia is not safe for Romans. Actually, it is not safe for anyone. That's why the people of my village are packing up as we speak—we are moving north to the lands of our kin, the Free Dacians."

"I think you are underestimating the strength of the legions."

"Ha, you legionaries think yourself to be invincible! So did Aquila, and look where it left me, alone and in danger of being lynched by zealots." Dochia turned her back on Strabo, but not before he could glimpse a couple of tears running down her cheeks.

"I am sorry," he said, not sure what he should be sorry for. "Aquila, was he your husband?"

She sighed deeply, shaking her head. "Yes, he was—Centurion Aquila, the former commander of the small garrison guarding the ruins. We were supposed to get officially married and settle down on our farm as soon as he got his *honesta missio*. But then, the civil war started, and he requested a transfer back to the legions."

"I…"

"The bloody, selfish idiot! 'I must defend the Empire,' he said. What about his duty to me?" Dochia shook with fury and frustration, so Strabo decided it would be wiser to say nothing.

"If you want to go north and die, go ahead. I am done saving your hide."

Strabo walked away from the campfire. If what Dochia said was true, he had to warn Pacatus of the danger and request immediate reinforcements from Apulum. He glanced back, reluctant to part ways in anger.

"Thank you for everything."

Dochia shrugged. "Just be gone already."

******

He followed a narrow footpath snaking between the tall trees. It led to the northwest, around the rocky outcrop he must have fallen off from. The going would have been easy under normal circumstances. However, he was still dizzy and weakened.

He lost track of time; it must have been around noon. The lush leaves of the spring forest shielded the sun. His stomach growled loudly, admonishing him for leaving Dochia without packing a few bites for the road. Strabo lost his canteen during the chase, so he had no water either.

At least I have my gladius. A legionary should die with a sword in hand, even if he dies of starvation.

Strabo marched on, listening for the sounds of gurgling water. In fact, he focused so much on finding something to drink that he totally disregarded the two armed men waiting for him down the path.

"Well, well, if it is not *Frumentarius* Strabo, the Emperor's cur."

He recognized the speaker as one of Blaesus' tent-mates; the other guy looked like a sheepherder. The two of them circled around Strabo, sword in hand.

I am fucked! It was the first thought flashing through Strabo's mind. On a good day, a trained legionary should have a fighting chance against a green auxilia and a civilian. But this wasn't a good day, not at all. Strabo was hungry, thirsty, and weak from the previous day's ordeal. His only chance was to distract them and then deal with them one at a time.

"I was looking forward to chatting with you again, Footman... Unfortunately, I forgot your name; I am sorry. I am not good at recalling all the traitors I have dispatched during working hours."

The deserter scoffed. "You'll remember me, alright, since I am the last person you'll ever see." He lunged forward with his sword, but his attack was sloppy. The movement of his feet pre-warned Strabo, so he had no trouble dodging it. *Pacatus and Dardanos did a shit job training their troops.*

Strabo was on the move, not allowing the other guy to fall behind him. If these two had been professionals, they would coordinate their attacks.

"You couldn't spear helpless Cotiso properly. What makes you think you can kill me?"

"Cotiso was not worthy, and Zalmoxis rejected him. If he had been a man, he should have taken his own worthless life instead of crawling back to the fort."

Sheepy tried an overhead blow, but he was too slow, and the Roman *gladius* he wielded was too short for these kinds of moves. Strabo effortlessly sidestepped the falling sword and stabbed his attacker—the steel point glanced off one of his ribs, protecting his lungs and heart from a fatal wound.

"Arrrrgggh!" The Dacian howled in pain. Now both of Strabo's adversaries were in front of him.

"You see, my friends, killing a legionary is not as easy as murdering that poor bastard, Blaesus." Strabo taunted them, hoping to prompt another mistake from these amateurs. Unfortunately, his last move made them cautious.

"Don't speak ill of him, cur! Zalmoxis accepted our message, deeming brother Blaesus worthy of his divine presence."

Strabo was confused. "What the fuck are you talking about?"

"Not another word, you Roman scum!"

At this, the ex-soldier thrust his sword at Strabo's belly while his Dacian companion attempted a slashing attack at his left side. Strabo deflected the deserter's thrust toward his companion, breaking the attacker's nose with a healthy elbow strike. The impact pushed the now-bleeding deserter into his hapless comrade, unbalancing him—Strabo took three steps forward and stabbed the deserter in the throat in one fluid motion. Blood erupted in all directions, sprinkling the remaining enemy's face with rust-brown droplets.

Surprisingly, Sheepy recovered his wits as soon as Strabo freed his *gladius* from his previous victim's ruined body. The Dacian charged headfirst, impervious to danger—

Strabo smiled to himself, knowing that the careless attack would allow him to finish the fight. However, Fortuna had a different outcome in mind.

As he tried to sidestep the charge, Strabo stumbled on a rotten tree trunk and fell flat on his back. The impact made him drop his gladius. A cruel, toothless grin split the face of Strabo's would-be executioner as he raised his blade for the killing blow. Strabo's last thought was a fitting epitaph for his funeral stone. *I lived like a fool, and I died like a fool!*

Alas, Sheepy's head jerked back as an arrow pierced one of his eyes. Strangely enough, he managed to regain his balance, standing there motionlessly, sword above his head, the gory remains trickling down his face. Strabo was too stunned to react. Finally, the guy dropped to his knees and fell forward, enveloping Strabo in a macabre embrace. The dying body shook with a final spasm, squeezing a struggling Strabo beneath.

"Oh...my...gods! What is this disgusting smell?" Strabo cried out as he tried to push the dead body off him.

"That, my delicate friend, is probably the smell of emptying bowels," Dochia said.

"Get him off me! Get him off!"

She ignored him, continuing her train of thought, "Mixed with the smell of layer after layer of sheep shit soaked in by his clothes over a lifetime of herding the fluffy little buggers."

Eventually, Strabo wriggled from below his victim's soiled body. "Disgusting!" Will this smell ever wash out? This tunic cost me a fortune, for gods' sake."

Dochia grinned. "Please, no hugs and kisses, ok? And try to stay downwind...at least five paces away from me."

Strabo shot her a withering look. She shrugged it off casually, then added, "Let's go. We should reach the fort before dusk."

IX. Cupid's Stealthy Arrow

They should be within sight of the fort any moment now. The pair walked silently for a couple of hours, ever vigilant for hostile elements. Then, finally, Dochia signaled for a short break, conjuring a piece of stale bread and a slice of cheese. Strabo took half of each, and they began their frugal supper.

"What will you do after reaching the fort?"

"I will dispatch couriers to request immediate reinforcements. A couple of legionary cohorts should do the trick. Meanwhile, we will consolidate our defenses and expand the camp to accommodate the extra troops once they arrive."

She was unconvinced. "I hope it will prove enough; many local men joined Decaeneus. I guess his army numbers in the thousands by now."

"Hmm, judging by those two," he pointed toward his back, "it's more like a rabble than an army."

"Don't underestimate the power of fanaticism."

As they finished their last morsels, a thought struck Strabo. "One of the zealots mentioned that Blaesus was a worthy messenger to Zalmoxis. Does this mean anything to you?"

Dochia took out the carved symbol hanging on her necklace and grabbed it with both hands. Strabo instantly recognized it.

"What's that? My mother has one just the same."

She arched her eyebrows questioningly. "Is she a local, then?" He nodded. "It is the symbol of Zalmoxis, the ancient god of the Dacians. Not many true believers are left, but most of us still wear these to ward off evil."

"I see. What about Blaesus?"

"Am I right to assume three spears pierced his body?" Her hand didn't leave the symbol. Strabo nodded again. "It is an ancient ritual our forefathers used to dispatch messages to Zalmoxis. Several men lifted one of the believers and threw him over three spears. If the messenger was worthy, he would be pierced by all three, and his soul would depart to the god."

Things began to make sense. Blaesus was selected as a messenger, which is why Strabo's mother suspected it was not murder.

"What if the messenger isn't killed during the ritual?"

"It would mean that the person is not worthy of Zalmoxis. At best, he would be an outcast. At worst, he would be lynched."

So Cotiso was a messenger wanna-be. He failed to die on the spears, so his companions beat him. It would explain the bruises on his face and body. And the utter fear emanating from him during the interrogation.

They resumed their journey as Strabo tried to digest his newfound knowledge.

"Do you know what message these looneys sent to Zalmoxis?"

"I can easily guess. They asked if the time had come to crush the Roman occupiers."

"And you think the answer was affirmative?"

"There is your answer," Dochia said, pointing toward the now-visible fort. A dark mass of howling men fanned out in front of the timber walls, brandishing swords, axes, and spears.

Strabo glanced sideways at his companion. Dochia's eyes betrayed genuine fear.

He was not a religious man, but being the target of some ancient god's wrath was not a comforting thought nonetheless, especially if the divine retribution took the form of an angry mob of lunatics.

******

"I need to get inside the fort."

"Are you insane? What are you hoping to accomplish?"

He grimaced, unsure. "That moron Pacatus couldn't win a fair fight, let alone overcome those unfavorable odds."

She scoffed. "And you think you can? You must have hit your head harder than I thought."

Pride hurt, he snapped. "Have a little faith, will you? I've spent five years fighting real soldiers and survived, haven't I? So I'll not be deterred by a bunch of sheep-loving, cousin-humping, shit-smelling bastards. Even a *gladius* through the eye couldn't stop me from walking away from Lugdunum."

His comments probably sounded harsher than he intended, for he could hear Dochia's sobs in the lightless night.

"Hey," he said softly, "I am sorry..."

"My husband, Aquila, died at Lugdunum. He died a hero, they said, sacrificing himself so his wounded men could be evacuated behind the lines."

Memories of the battle flashed through Strabo's mind. It was a massacre at a scale never seen before. Roman against Roman, *frater versus frater*, pitted against each other by the all-consuming ambition of their leaders. Luckily for Strabo, the man he fought for eventually prevailed, securing his claim to the Imperial Purple. But, the tides shifted many times during the two-day battle, and Septimius Severus could have lost just as easily as he won—Strabo would be dead now, and no one would have been surprised by the outcome. Despite being victorious, countless thousands of

Severus' troops paid the ultimate price, Dochia's husband among them.

He reached out, trying to offer some comfort. She slapped his hand away.

"There are some ancient tunnels dug beneath the fort. Aquila discovered them while looking for ways to sneak out to visit me."

"Does anybody else know about them?" Strabo said, worried the rebels might use them to breach the defenses.

"No, I don't think so. I'll show you to the hidden entrance, and then, you are on your own."

They circled the besieging forces through the south. Dochia led them on seldom-used forest paths Strabo would have difficulties spotting even during daylight. He followed as carefully as he could, freezing motionlessly at her signals. She was alert, listening for sounds of enemy patrols. The stillness of the night was disturbed only by the occasional hooting owl or the rustles of a scurrying rodent. Once she decided the path ahead was clear, they carried on. Eventually, they reached a creek lazily flowing between rocky outcrops.

Dochia stepped into the shallow but ice-cold water gesturing for him to follow.

It is cold! He mentally cursed when his feet became instantly numb.

She guided him upstream to where the towering cliff walls choked the river, speeding its flow. His companion pointed at a dark hole gaping at the foot of one of the rock faces. "Through there. Follow the main tunnel, and always keep right at the crossroads."

Strabo moved his gaze between the cave entrance and Dochia, not sure what to say.

I hate farewells.

The moon emerged between the clouds, blanketing the entire landscape in its silvery light. Her emerald-green eyes draw him closer and closer in some sort of mystical attraction. Before he even realized it, Strabo leaned forward and kissed her. Surprisingly, Dochia returned his kiss with unexpected passion before pushing him away. "I can't lose another foolish Roman. Go!"

Oblivious to the dangers of being overheard, he shouted at her departing shape, "After all this is over, look me up in Sarmizegetusa. Ask for Aquilina's *insula*." She disappeared into the night.

X. A Fort in Disarray

Strabo had to crawl on all fours for several dozen feet before the entrance opened into a large tunnel. A pair of dry torches hung on the wall-mounted sockets, a piece of flint on the rusty shelf below. *Did Aquila leave these, or had somebody else discovered the tunnels?*

He lit one of the torches and looked around. It seemed that the cave complex was a natural formation. He advanced carefully to avoid slipping on the humid floor. The path went straight for a while, and most of it could be comfortably traversed. He had to duck only now and then to avoid hitting his head on the low-hanging ceiling. Finally, Strabo reached the first intersection, where the gallery split three ways. The right branch had an ochre-red arrow painted above it, while the other two were unmarked.

Follow the right direction, he recalled Dochia's instructions.

A quarter of an hour and three more intersections later, Strabo reached a dead-end. He leaned forward, using his torch to light the wall blocking his way—torch sockets were mounted on it, suggesting a hidden exit somewhere. He leaned onto the rocky surface ahead and pushed; it moved with surprising ease.

The fake wall must have been mounted on wheels.

Strabo extinguished his torch and placed it beside the others before carefully exiting the cave. Although it was dark, Strabo could distinguish the shapes of wooden barrels stored all over the place.

I am below the fort's warehouse, he guessed.

Strabo closed the secret passage behind him and looked for a ladder leading out of the cellar. He climbed, opened the trap door, and stepped into the warehouse's ground floor. A faint light came in from under the building's large gates. Strabo tried to open them, but they wouldn't budge.

Of course, they were locked from the outside.

"Open the door!" he yelled, banging his fists on the gates. "Somebody, open the fucking door!"

Shouted voices could be heard outside. Strabo kept banging and screaming, hoping one of the soldiers would eventually hear him. He could make out the anxious voice from the door's other side. "They are in the warehouse! Torch the building, and let them burn like rats!"

"No, no, no! You moron, it is me, *Frumentarius* Strabo! Just open the bloody gate!"

Heavy footsteps approached while Strabo continued in an increasingly desperate tone, "Don't set the building on fire! Call Pacatus at once! Do you hear? Call Pacatus! It is an order!"

Trickles of sweat ran down Strabo's back as he considered an unceremonious exit via the secret tunnels. Finally, the gates opened with a loud creak—two dozen soldiers formed a shield wall, blocking his way.

"I am *Frumentarius* Lucius Lucretius Strabo. I was here earlier investigating the death of Footman Blaesus. You might remember me."

"What in the name of the gods are you doing in there?" An anxious Pacatus pushed himself forward through the ranks. "Were you sleeping in the warehouse all this time?"

Strabo rolled his eyes. It seemed Pacatus' brainpower decreased further when under pressure.

"There is a hidden tunnel beneath the warehouse. But, never mind that; I need to talk to you. In private."

"Hidden…what?"

"In your office. Now!"

Strabo walked past the confused Centurion and toward the command building.

******

Strabo summarized his findings—the sacrificial ritual conducted by Decaeneus ending in Blaesus' death, the reason for Cotiso's murder, and the religious motivations of the deserters.

Pacatus was dispirited, and his shaking hands mirrored his inner fears.

"But what do they want from us?" the Centurion squeaked.

Strabo shrugged. "They would like us to die or, at least, leave their lands, I guess."

"*Their* lands?"

"The lands which belonged to their forefathers. Come on! You know what I meant."

The Centurion nodded apologetically. "Still, why the fort?"

"Why not? What does it matter anyway?" Strabo struggled to control his annoyance. "Have they stated their demands?"

"No, nothing. They came out of the woods yesterday, pitching their camp and blocking our exit."

Hmm, that was strange. Why wouldn't they attack? Or share their demands? Maybe they are waiting for something.

"Have you prepared our defenses?"

"O-o-of course. All the men are on the walls, ready in case of an assault."

"The men have been on the walls since yesterday?"

Pacatus hesitated. "Any other suggestions?" The commander's eyes practically begged Strabo to intervene.

"Have you sent for reinforcements, as I said?"

"Well…errr…there was no time, you see…." Pacatus left the thought hanging.

Strabo took a deep calming breath before barking out his instructions, "First, you should rest half the men. At this rate, they will be dead-tired by the time of the assault. Got it?"

"Yes, of course."

"So, what are you waiting for? Order four *contubernia* to rest until dawn. And then rotate them. The others should rest while the fresh soldiers guard the fort. Go, now!"

Strabo remained alone in the office, trying to think things through. They couldn't hold out for long; that much was clear. But, if they escaped using the tunnels, Decaeneus and his rabble would move on, ransacking the unprotected Roman villas and farms.

Oh no! Father and Mother are only a day's march from here.

The longer the fort defenders held out, the more time the colonists had to flee and for the legions to muster. But only if they were aware of the incoming danger.

Strabo walked out briskly, following in the steps of the Centurion. He went to the wall asking loudly for all the gathered men to hear, "Who is the swiftest runner among you?"

A skinny boy, barely out of his childhood, timidly raised his hand. Strabo gestured for him to get down.

"What is your name?" he said softly.

"Philipos, sir!"

"I have a critical mission for you, Philipos, one that can save countless lives. But first, go to the *cantina*, fetch something to eat, and pack food for the road. Then, when you are done, wait for me in front of the warehouse."

"Road, sir?" Strabo's severe posture discouraged further questions. "Yes, sir!"

After the boy left, Strabo hoofed it to the sick bay.

"Tardus? Where the hell are you?" He shouted into the dark sick bay. The half-sleeping *capsarius* came out of his room yawning.

"Stand at attention!" Strabo was furious. "Are you aware we are under siege?"

"Y-y-yes."

"I can't hear you, you lazy bastard!"

"Yes, sir!"

"So why are you sleeping instead of preparing for casualties?"

"Well, nobody said..."

"Listen to me very carefully, Tardus, for I shall say this only once," Strabo hissed. A loud swallowing sound followed Tardus' nod. "You will prepare all the beds, including the ones in the back and your room—we need as many beds as possible for the wounded. Then, you will fill the water buckets and prepare the bandages, the ointments, and everything else you might need. Am I clear?"

"Yes, sir!"

"Good. When you are done, you come and report to me. I'll allocate two servants as orderlies—their job will be to carry the wounded to the sick bay. Carry on, *Capsarie!*"

Next, Strabo looked for the quartermaster. Finally, he identified the round, soft man standing guard on one of the walls.

"You, Fatty! Yes, you; come down immediately!" The soldiers on the wall looked down, confused to hear somebody giving orders. But Strabo's bluff worked because men craved leadership, especially during uncertain times—as long as he sounded confident, people would follow him.

"Grab half of the tent servants and bring out every single throwing spear you can find. Line them up here, so you can easily hand them to the men on the wall."

"Understood, sir!"

"Wait! Do we have any flammables?"

The quartermaster scratched his chin before answering, "Yes, sir. We have several buckets of the pitch we use for insulation."

"Perfect, hand them out on the wall, one bucket to each *contubernia*. What about kindling? Do we store wooden sticks?"

"Yes, sir, we do."

"Good; after you finish with the *pila*, start preparing faggots."

"Faggots, sir?"

"Are you deaf or something? Faggots! As in bundles of sticks bound together. We can light them up and rain them on the assaulting enemy."

"Yes, sir! Very well, sir!"

"Dismissed!"

Lastly, the men had to eat.

Half of his teeth gone, the army cook was an old, spindly man.

"Gran'pa, how long will our supplies last?"

"Longer than these fat bastards, that's for sure." He cackled.

At least somebody had some sense.

"They will last even less if starved to death," Strabo said pointedly. "What about water? Do we have enough?"

"Yep."

"Care to elaborate?"

"And they call you a special agent, eh? You are more like a special needs agent, I reckon." He spat before continuing, "Look there, *Domine*, do you see that well?" Strabo saw it— truth be told, he used it during his previous visit, but the fact slept his tired mind.

"Ok, Gramps, point taken." Strabo raised his hands apologetically. "Listen, I need your help. We will rotate the men every four hours—you must put some warm food into 80 starving men's bellies six times a day. You should feed the incoming shift first; once they take their place on the wall, you feed the outgoing shift. Got it?"

"I am old, not dumb."

"Take the remaining tent servants; they'll help you." Strabo turned to leave, then remembered. "Add some *posca* to the menu for the fresh shift, will you?"

"Any other drops of wisdom you want to share with your grandpa?"

Strabo laughed, releasing some of the accumulated tension. "I apologize. I didn't want to offend you. It is just that…"

"…that Pacatus and the others are fucking morons?" He turned and went about his business, not waiting for Strabo's answer.

Now that he arranged for the men to be fed, rested, armed to the teeth, and patched up, there was one last thing he had to do—make sure their sacrifice was not in vain.

Philipos waited anxiously in front of the warehouse. Strabo opened the gate and led him in, a lit torch in hand. Philipos followed down the ladder and to the hidden door. A couple of small cracks allowed Strabo to pull the fake wall, opening the catacombs' entrance.

"Those tunnels lead to a westward exit," Strabo told the breathless boy. "As soon as you are outside, run as fast as you can. By noon, you should reach the legionary post guarding the crossroads between the Imperial highway and the road leading to our gods' forsaken fort. Ask them to send a courier to Camp Praefect Hilarius of the Thirteenth Legion with a message from *Frumentarius* Lucius Strabo.

Philipos nodded. "What's the message?"

"Two thousand Dacian rebels besiege the fort guarding Sarmizegetusa Regia. Hilarius is to raise three cohorts and march them immediately to our support. Meanwhile, we'll try to hold out for a few days, despite being significantly outnumbered."

"I understand, sir. But…," Philipos said, unsure if he should continue.

"Go on, then."

"Why are we not evacuating the fort through these tunnels?"

"As long as we hold out, the rebels will be kept in one place, unable to wreak havoc through the province. However, those lunatics will spread out if we leave, destroying and killing civilians while gathering new supporters emboldened by their victory here. Before we know it, Decaeneus will have an army of tens of thousands."

"I see."

"If things turn desperate, we'll evacuate. But we need to buy time for the reinforcements to arrive."

"How much time do we need, sir?"

Strabo shook his head. "I am afraid we need more than we have. Now, off you go!"

XI. An Offer One Can't Refuse

After a few hours of shut-eye, Strabo woke up to a well-organized camp as his earlier instructions were successfully executed. The men on the wall were eager and rested, weapons at the ready. Simultaneously, the crooked old cook was like fish in the water, pushing the servants around to clean everything and prepare the meal for the following change of the guard. Even Tardus did a marvelous job setting up the hospital for the oncoming slaughter.

"Look who decided to join the living," the wicked chef said. "Here, have some gruel and a cup of *posca*; it'll wake you up."

Strabo remembered the first time he tasted the *posca*—a mix of warm vinegary wine and water consumed by soldiers all over the Empire as a pick-me-up. Strabo thought it was horrible then, but after half a year of binge drinking with his friend Porcius, it tasted ok.

He walked up the wall, trying to figure out the enemy's disposition. The rebels were not an army—clearly, they lacked the necessary training and discipline. The two thousand or so men slept scattered on the ground in a disorderly mass. Some walked about sick from the previous night's drinking, trying to find something to ease the hangover. It didn't seem like they planned an assault.

What are they waiting for?

"*Tesserarie!*" He called for the watch commander. "Report!"

"Nothing out of the ordinary, sir. They drank until late morning, according to the previous shift's commander. Then, some got into a drunken brawl. Eventually, most of them passed out."

"We might even survive this, *Tesserarie*."

The junior officer smiled at this. "Yes, sir. We might."

"Let me know if there are any changes."

With that said, Strabo visited the *capsarius* for a long-overdue change of his bandages. As Tardus worked on his head, Strabo fell into a dreamless sleep.

******

"Strabo, wake up!"

"Whaaat? Where am I?"

"Your rebel priest is here," Pacatus said, wriggling his hands anxiously.

Strabo jumped out of bed, sprinkled his face with cold water from one of the buckets, and darted out of the sick bay. From the top of the wall, they could see that the rebel camp bustled with sudden activity at the exhortations of Decaeneus. A group of men in scarlet guarded the Dacian priest, and Strabo guessed they were *Optio* Dardanus and the deserters.

So they were waiting for Decaeneus.

An hour later, the entire rebel mob deployed in more or less orderly rows in front of the main gate and the adjacent wall. Eventually, the priest and his guard approached the gates and stopped two dozen feet away.

"I am Decaeneus, the High Priest of Zalmoxis and the Herald of His return!" the man declaimed in a booming voice. "I demand to speak with the Roman commander!"

Strabo looked at Pacatus, gesturing for him to speak up. The Centurion, however, deferred to Strabo. "Well, you are the Emperor's representative. Technically this leaves you in charge."

Pacatus' assertion was flawed; as a *frumentarius,* Strabo had no authority to lead the troops. However, he was unwilling to show weakness in front of the troops.

"Ah, the old men from the ruins. To what do we owe the pleasure of your visit?"

Decaeneus shot a glance at Dardanos. His unspoken reprimand was unmistakable even from a distance, *'You told me he was dead.'* The former *Optio* avoided the priest's gaze.

"So the defiler of our ancient temple is alive." A cruel smile split the priest's bearded face. "My *barbarian* brothers!" He gestured at the defending auxilia. "Leave now, and I am guaranteeing safe passage to Apulum for every one of you. All I am asking in return is that you entrust your Roman masters' lapdog," he pointed his oaken staff at Strabo, "to our good care."

All eyes on the wall turned to Strabo, and he could feel the calculating thoughts behind those looks. Except for a few officers, the auxiliary troops were not Roman citizens. Why would they choose almost certain death when they could escape with the loss of a single man, an arrogant Roman who looks down on them as mere *barbarians*?

Strabo knew his following words could mean the end of his short life, but dragging on the silence would surely condemn him. He had no choice but to gamble.

"Do you honestly believe that real soldiers would run away in fear of this rabble of yours?" He gestured at the rag-tag rebel lines. "Besides, my mother is Dacian, and my father was born in Dacia. So, I am as much a provincial as any of these boys." He glanced left and right, trying to gauge the effect of his words. "We never leave one of ours behind. Are we, boys?"

The silence dragged on for what seemed like an eternity. Meanwhile, Strabo contemplated a fate worse than death.

"Of course, we don't!" the old cook shattered the deafening stillness. "You can shove that stick of yours up your backside until you can sample its wooden taste." The irreverent comment elicited a good laugh, dispelling the tension.

Strabo sighed, relieved. "I believe you have your answer, Decaeneus. I suggest you disperse your band of lunatics before the reinforcements from Apulum arrive. Praefect Hilarius might even be in the mood to overlook this transgression and settle for only a dozen or so crucifixions. One can always hope." He grinned.

Decaeneus was not amused. "We will wash away the filth from Zalmoxis' house by spilling your blood on its hallowed grounds. So, say your final prayers to whatever gods you worship, for this is your last chance to do it."

The rebel priest turned, and his guards followed on his heels. Strabo was alive for now, but it seemed unlikely that the old cook could save him from what was about to come.

XII. A Fiery Trap

The defenders spent the day preparing for the inevitable onslaught. Strabo rested most of the men, leaving only a *contubernia* on the wall at any given time. The other four tents of each shift relaxed on the ground, ready to man the timber palisade as soon as the enemy made any threatening move.

Decaeneus' rebels were busy too. They cut down a massive tree and used its trunk to build a crude battering ram. Others used the branches to fashion several assault ladders—Strabo counted twenty of them, enough to assault the small fort from all directions and stretch out the defenders. *And then they'll use the battering ram.* It was a simple yet effective plan, Strabo had to admit.

"Pacatus, do we have caltrops by any chance?"

The Centurion scratched his head, trying to remember. "Well, this fort hasn't seen action since the Marcommanic invasion. Still...You two!" The commander pointed at a couple of soldiers. "Search the warehouse's cellar for anything useful—those trunks and crates have been untouched for decades."

Fortuna smiled upon them, for they found several crates full of rusty caltrops, old *amphorae* of rancid oil, and old but usable spears—all of these could be put to good use.

The caltrops were designed so that one of their three spikes always pointed upwards. The unlucky fellow stepping on any of them would be instantly taken out of combat. Moreover, the wound would probably fester, given the rust on the decades-old caltrop stock, leading to a slow, painful death.

A very Roman contraption, the caltrop—brutal yet effective.

From a strategic perspective, inflicting a debilitating injury was far better than killing instantly—the wounded combatants had to be cared for, tying down precious resources and slowing down the enemy's advance. Also, watching the sufferings of their comrades can deal a blow to the opposing side's morale.

Suspecting Decaeneus' plan to encircle the fort and assault it from all directions, Strabo instructed his soldiers to discreetly sow the ground around the defenses with caltrops except for the area in front of the gate. He hoped to funnel the enemy through a bottleneck, thus minimizing their overwhelming numerical superiority.

Additionally, the defenders used some of the old spears to assemble kinds of pitchforks; these could be used to push away the enemy's assault ladders.

As soon as darkness fell, Strabo lowered a handful of soldiers down the walls. They poured the rancid oil and the pitch onto the grounds fronting the gate.

"Do you think your plan will work?" Pacatus said, his voice betraying an ill-concealed fear.

"I think we will be able to delay them long enough to doom their rebellion."

Pacatus scoffed. "How can you be so sure Hilarius will send reinforcements? Is he even aware of our predicament?"

Strabo put his hands on the Centurion's shoulder. He could feel his companion's trembling, confirming Pacatus' unfitness for his role once again.

"Trust me, will you?" Strabo tried to reassure the poor fellow. "We will hold them up for a day or two. We might even cripple their rag-tag little band so that the reinforcements could mop them up easily."

The commander sighed, not entirely convinced. "That's all well and proper, but what about us? Will we survive?"

Strabo shrugged, wondering about the same thing. *Will I see Dochia again?* The thought took him by surprise, but he forgave himself for fantasizing about the ravishing huntress as he might not have another chance to let his imagination run wild.

******

An eerie stillness blanketed the enemy's camp; it was a far cry compared to the previous night's revelry. Moreover, the cloudy sky obstructed the moonlight, and the whole landscape was covered in darkness. Strabo suspected the rebels might use this to their advantage and attempt a surprise assault, so he ordered the entire Century onto the encircling walls. In addition, he armed the tent servants with the improvised pitchforks—although they lacked training and armor, the long contraptions might allow them to keep the ladders off the defenses.

The hours went by slowly, the tension floating in the air. The Roman auxiliaries were surprisingly disciplined—except for the occasional muffled cough, no one breached the—

"Aaaaa!" A blood-curdling cry pierced the night, coming from the northern side. It was followed by other shouts of pain as more rebels stepped into the caltrops. With their stealthy approach failing, the enemy ranks broke into a charge.

"Light the faggots!" Strabo shouted.

The burning bundles of sticks were thrown over the wall, illuminating the enemy's movements. The rebels swarmed on all sides, grouped around their fellows carrying the ladders. More rebels fell as the spiky traps maimed their feet. Eventually, the northern charge faltered, the attackers reluctant to advance, wary of the traps.

"*Pila* at the ready!" The men raised the infamous Roman throwing spears.

"Aim at twenty feet!" The auxilia leaned back and drew their arms, ready to throw.

"Lose!"

Since the rebels were massed together, the overwhelming majority of the spears hit home, skewering countless unarmored attackers. The same scene played out on the western and southern sides. However, the enemy approaching the gates advanced unhindered—Strabo specifically instructed his men to allow the enemy to reach the gate with the battering ram.

As a result, the rebels abandoned the side assaults and converged on the front gate, where their comrades seemed to be close to a breakthrough. This movement was mirrored on the Roman side, with Strabo ordering the men to bolster the gate defenses.

So far, so good.

"Boom!" The battering ram's blow shook the entire wooden fort.

"Hold the gate!" Pacatus encouraged his men to lean against the gate and soften the next blow.

"Boom!"

"Light them up, Strabo! What the fuck are you waiting for?" The Centurion waved at Strabo, trying to get his attention, as the situation at the gate became increasingly dire.

Strabo glanced around, timing his order for maximum effect. The rebels managed to climb the ladders and jump on the wall in a couple of places. They pushed back the defenders just enough for more of their comrades to be able to join. In most instances, though, the Romans pushed back the ladders, crashing them down on the rebel mass.

"Boom!" A score of muscular men maneuvered the massive tree trunk, continuing to bang against the creaking doors. Behind them, a thousand howling Dacians pushed against each other in their frantic desire to breach the fort.

"Crispus, light the fuckers up!" Strabo nodded toward his field aid. The junior officer lit the torch and casually threw it on the oil-soaked ground swarming with enemies. What followed would haunt Strabo for a long time.

The flames engulfed the Dacians almost instantly. The howls of agony mixed with the cries of those desperately trying to get out of the fire's range. The massed ranks of their comrades blocked their escape, so many ran heedlessly into the caltrops fields, choosing the slow death of a festering wound to the horrifying one of being burned alive.

"Aim at those in the back!" Strabo pointed. Four dozen *pila* rained down on those who managed to get out of the inferno. More waves followed, piercing the unprotected bodies—heads and chests exploded, blood and gore splashing left and right.

The whole scene lasted less than a quarter of an hour. The stench of charred flesh was overpowering. Still, Strabo could distinguish the metallic tang of blood and the rotten smell of soiled corpses.

He took in the scene below the gate as a cold rain slowly cleared the smoke. The blackened remains of a thousand men littered the ground, a couple of hundreds more lying motionless, spears protruding out of their bodies. The grievously wounded moaned as they clung to what remained of their lives while some slowly crawled out of the fort's range, their feet rendered useless by the Roman traps.

"What a waste," Strabo whispered, shaking his head sadly.

"Sir!" Crispus' voice interrupted. "Over there! We trapped some of them."

Strabo jumped down into the fort's courtyard and ran toward the unfolding scene. Some of those rebels who climbed the walls earlier were trapped inside the sick bay. A score of auxilia blocked the exit of the building while a couple of men in scarlet tunics faced them from the other side.

"Report," Strabo said to the man in charge.

"The traitor Dardanos and some of his deserters are inside. They threaten to kill our wounded and *Capsarius* Tardus if we attempt to take the sick bay by storm."

"How many are they?"

"Five or six."

Strabo nodded, then shouted for those inside to hear him, "Dardanos, it doesn't have to end this way."

"Not a step forward!" came the reply through one of the windows. "One more step, and I'll butcher the hostages."

"Why are you doing this, Dardanos? Those people were under your command for years. Have you no honor?"

"You should have left when you had the chance. No one had to die today." Dardanos' voice broke. "It is all your fault!"

"Come out, and I'll grant you and your men safe passage."

"Decaeneus will be back soon. This time there's no escape for you, Strabo." Dardanos let out a hysterical laugh.

Something is not right.

Strabo tried to prod Dardanos to reveal their plan. "Half of your rebel army is dead, and the other half is in disarray, scared shitless. There is no way the old fool can coerce the survivors to make another attempt."

Dardanos leaned out of the window, and Strabo saw a sad smile on his face. "You don't understand, do you? This place," he gestured, "is the key to everything. Once Decaeneus performs the ritual, all Dacia will rise and crush the Romans once and for all." As he spoke, a loud thud came from inside the building.

"What the hell!" Dardanos began to turn when the tip of a blade came out of his neck in an explosion of blood. Tardus' grinning face emerged as he removed the scalpel from his victim's bleeding wound. Seizing the moment, Crispus and his men stormed the entrance, quickly dispatching the remaining deserters.

Still dazzled by the events, Strabo stepped inside, trying to understand what had happened.

"Tardus?"

"Thank you for creating the distraction, sir. While you chatted them up, the boys and I," he pointed toward the wounded in the back, "took them by surprise."

"Good work," Strabo said, unable to escape the feeling that Dardanos died moments before he could shed light on this whole business.

What kind of horrific ritual could shatter the Empire?

XIII. Zalmoxis Revealed

"You knew about these catacombs all along? Why didn't you tell me?" Pacatus was apoplectic.

Strabo shrugged. "I did tell you, remember? How do you think I landed inside the warehouse the other day?" Strabo crossed his arms over his chest defiantly. "Anyway, what would you have done differently? Eh?"

"Evacuate, of course. Save our men."

"Our duty is to defend Rome with our lives. So, as long as we could inflict heavy losses and nip this whole rebellion in the bud, we had to stay."

"Twenty of our men died, and over a dozen are wounded."

"Twenty of ours and a thousand of theirs. I'd say it was a good trade-off." Strabo was unable to hide his disdain. He said, "Look, Centurion, if you can't stomach taking tough decisions, maybe you should find yourself another line of work. Now, quit wasting time and begin the evacuation! Wounded first, servants next, followed by the rest of the Century, one tent at a time—the tunnels are too narrow for a mass evacuation. I'll stay with the last *contubernia*, keeping an eye out for the enemy." With that said, Strabo stormed out and joined Crispus and a handful of soldiers on the walls.

Strabo looked away because he couldn't bear the sight of the countless dead rebels anymore. He decided to use the opportunity provided by the relative peace and rewind the whole case in his head.

A fanatical Dacian priest returned from exile to stir up a rebellion against Rome. Under his influence, several Roman auxilia of Thracian and Dacian descent participated in an occult ritual to contact their long-lost god, Zalmoxis, and ask for divine support.

Footman Cotiso volunteered as a messenger but failed to die on the three spears as he should have. The fanatics took this as a sign of unworthiness and nearly beat Cotiso to death. Still, the unlucky guy managed to crawl back to the fort and get medical help from Tardus.

The second volunteer, Blaesus, was successful and died appropriately during the ceremony, signaling Zalmoxis' blessing for the rebellion. When a Roman patrol found the body of their colleague, they mistakenly concluded that he was murdered. Enter Strabo.

The turncoats realized Cotiso would break under Strabo's expert interrogation, so they distracted him and hanged Cotiso. Their actions, however, precipitated their plans.

Now that they revealed themselves as traitors, Dardanos and company deserted their posts, prompting Decaeneus to begin the rebellion without the advantage of spies within the Roman ranks.

This turn of events explained why the rebels waited in front of the fort for a few days and were ill-prepared for an assault.

The only unanswered question was, *why the fort?* Why was this place sacred? How could performing a ritual on its grounds spark a mass revolt in Dacia?

Strabo looked around the place, observing the different wooden buildings. *What secrets are hidden here?* Then, out of a sudden, the obvious hit him—the catacombs!

"I think I saw movement behind those bushes," one of the soldiers said, pointing toward a spot a few hundred feet ahead.

"We should go," Strabo said. "Pacatus had enough time to get everybody in the tunnels."

Strabo led his small party into the catacombs. As they reached the first crossroad, they could hear the steps of their comrades further down the corridors

"Crispus, stay here with the men and block any incoming enemy. The narrow passage is easily defendable. Buy

Pacatus as much time as possible and then retreat that way." Strabo pointed at the appropriate corridor.

"What about you, sir?" a confused Crispus said.

"I have some exploring to do. If possible, wait for me. If not…I will find a way out, don't worry."

Strabo took the other passage, the unmarked one. As he advanced, he noticed some strange symbols painted on the cave's walls. The color faded over the years, and the marks were barely visible in some places.

These must have been centuries old.

He pushed on through the thick spider webs and into a large opening—it seemed to be a kind of ceremonial hall. At the back of it was a sort of stone altar flanked by two massive vessels filled with what Strabo guessed was oil. He used the torch to light them up.

The flames' warm light revealed an impressive painting on the wall behind the altar. It depicted a well-built, naked man raising a huge double-edged ax above his head, ready for a blow.

"Impressive, isn't it?" Strabo jumped at the sound of the now-familiar voice. He turned to see Decaeneus and a dozen of his men entering the hall.

"Well, I would say the proportions are not exactly harmonious." Strabo pointed at the painting. "You see, his manhood is rather under-represented compared to the massive body. Is this why you guys are so angry?"

"Romans!" The priest spat. "Defiant to the end. However, I am glad that you are here. I believe it was ordained for the Ax of Zalmoxis to taste Roman blood for the first time in this sacred place." A cruel smile split the old man's bearded face. "Any last wishes?"

"Since I am to die here, at least you could do me the courtesy of explaining all this."

Decaeneus nodded. "A surprisingly worthy request. As you wish." He cleared his throat before saying, "Born a man, Zalmoxis was taken as a slave to Greece many centuries ago. He lived on the island of Samos, serving the famous Pythagoras—I assume you heard of him."

"I confess I was never good at philosophy despite having a criminally good teacher." Strabo thought of his previous case, the murder of the fake-philosopher Cleomoenes by a philosophically inclined legionary surgeon.

The priest ignored Strabo's comment and carried on with the story, "After being freed, Zalmoxis used his education to enrich himself. Then, he returned to his native lands of Dacia, where he built an impressive banquet hall. Next, he invited all the notables of Dacia and Thracia to a lavish banquet. Once everybody gathered for the feast, Zalmoxis told his guests that neither they nor their descendants would ever die if they followed his teachings. Instead, they would eventually go to a place where they would live forever, in a state of eternal happiness."

"Same old story, different con artist."

"After the banquet, Zalmoxis built an underground residence where he secretly retreated for three long years." The priest opened his arms in an embracing gesture, implying that the cave was the residence of the story. "The people were worried by Zalmoxis' disappearance, but once he miraculously returned during the fourth year, they embraced him as their god and his promise of a happy after-life."

"Promise eternal life in return for subservience, vanish, and then be reborn as a god. Neat."

"You mock us, but don't your emperors do the same? Become gods after their death?"

"I had the chance to meet our current divine ruler. Trust me; there is nothing godlike about him. He is but an ambitious soldier with leadership skills and a bit of luck."

"And still you have the Imperial Cult, worshipping dead emperors. Why is that?"

"The masses need rules and gods to enforce them. Otherwise, society falls apart."

"Precisely! And this is what Zalmoxis provided to the people of these lands. A god to worship and a set of rules to follow. Was he a god or just a visionary man? I don't know, and it doesn't matter. What matters is that his guidance led to a powerful Thracian kingdom when your beloved Rome was nothing more than an insignificant village. The subsequent rulers of Dacia were so powerful that they challenged the Persian Empire, Alexander's Macedonians, and even the almighty Roman Empire. And all of this was made possible by the unifying power of the Zalmoxian religion."

"And you are about to revive it and rally the people around it. How?"

"Look behind you, at the altar."

An ornate ax similar to the one wielded by the man in the painting was placed on the altar.

"Behold the Ax of Zalmoxis! After I chop your head off with it, I will announce to the world that our ancient god has finally returned to the cave of his initial transformation. And he entrusted to me his mighty ax, commanding me to lead his people against the Roman invaders."

Strabo scoffed. "You really believe the locals would follow you based on some convoluted story about a centuries-old divinity?"

"You said you are half-Dacian. Does your mother worship Zalmoxis?"

Strabo's face must have given him away, for Decaeneus smiled. "Do you see now? The Dacians and Thracians never forgot the old religion. They just buried it below the surface."

Losing ground, Strabo tried another counter. "Provided you are correct, and some fools would eventually follow your deluded gambit, how do you plan to defeat the legions? A mere century of auxiliaries repulsed ten times their numbers. Imagine what the fifteen thousand legionaries stationed in Dacia could do."

Decaeneus pursed his lips as he struggled to formulate his thoughts. He eventually said, "I have dedicated a lifetime to studying your Empire, looking for the right moment to strike. Ask yourself this, how secure is Septimius Severus on the throne? The last civil war ended barely a year ago. The legions are spread thin, ambitious men lurking in the shadows, waiting for their chance to grab the Imperial

Purple. It is only a question of time until Roman rule collapses, and then Dacia will be free again. I merely aim to speed up the process."

Despite himself, Strabo felt a growing admiration for the old man. Decaeneus was not the fanatic he seemed to be. On the contrary, he was a shrewd politician with a realistic plan to bring the mightiest empire the world has ever known to its knees.

"As much as I enjoyed our little conversation, there are pressing matters I have to attend to. So, be a good sacrificial sheep and try not to make this more difficult than it has to be." The Dacian priest signaled for his men to subdue Strabo.

Suddenly the noise of fighting came from the tunnels behind Decaeneus. Several legionaries led by a Roman officer poured into the hall, hacking and slashing as they advanced. Decaeneus pushed Strabo aside and reached for the ax on the altar. He raised it above his head, ready to strike. "In the name of divine Zalmoxis, I...." Before he could finish the sentence, the Roman officer stabbed him through the heart, then kicked him in the stomach, removing his bloody *gladius*.

"How many times do I need to save your ass, Stinky?" Hilarius' white grin contrasted with his blood-covered face. Strabo sighed, suspecting he'd soon regret that Decaeneus hadn't chopped his head off.

******

"Do you honestly expect me to believe these sheep-fuckers could destroy the Roman Empire?"

"Sir, as I explained before, religion can be powerful—"

"Bla bla bla! I killed the bastard on the altar of his god. If this 'Moxis guy was so powerful, why didn't he stop me?" Hilarius slapped Strabo on the back. "I have to admit, though, that you did a good job defending the fort and keeping the rebels in one place. Can we go home now?"

"I suggest we collapse the cave with everything in it, sir. No one should ever use it as a rallying point for further rebellion."

"Good thinking, son. Let me handle it."

As the Praefect left to give the necessary orders, Decaeneus' words kept ringing in Strabo's ears.

Was he right? Is the Roman Empire losing its grip on Dacia?

Strabo couldn't help but recall the famous words of Cicero, "*Male parta male dilabuntur.* What has been wrongly gained is wrongly lost."

Ave, Lector!

First of all, thank you for purchasing '*Male Parta: An Agent Strabo Mystery Novella.*'

I know you could have picked any number of books to read, but you chose this book, and for that, I am incredibly grateful.

If you enjoyed it and found some benefit in reading this, I'd like to hear from you and hope you could take some time to post a review on Amazon.

Your feedback and support will help me to improve my writing craft for future projects.

Thank you,

Alex

Books by the Author

The Martyr: A Roma Invicta Story (Book #1)

The "*Roma Invicta*" stories scrutinize the Ancient Roman civilization through the lens of alternate history. Blending historical fiction with sci-fi elements, the novella-length tales reflect the author's well-known style: long enough to be immersive but not to the extent of slowing down the pace.

What if the Roman Empire never fell?

Two thousand seven hundred and seventy-three years after the Founding of Rome, the Empire is stronger than ever. Peace and stability have reigned on Earth for centuries while the invincible legions extend the Pax Romana one star system at a time. However, unseen cracks appear under the façade of invincibility as long-forbidden ideas return to haunt the Empire.

When Marcus Amelius Pius embarks on a transformative journey, the Inquisition sends its best agent to apprehend him. Can Pius awaken the beliefs that once shook the Empire? Or will Inquisitor Ferox prevail?

Step into the alternate universe of "*The Martyr*" to find out!

The Growing Shadow: The City of Kings (Book #1)

Visions of the End Times are haunting the feverish dreams of a dying monk.

Rumors of strange attacks are reported by the patrols of the Northern border.

Trouble is brewing among the great lords of the kingdom as old enemies are requesting refuge against the growing shadow from the East.

Welcome to the City of Kings at the dawn of the First Mongol Invasion of Europe.

Delve into a story of lords and ladies, noble knights and ruthless warriors, mysterious and exotic adversaries, courtly scheming, religious strife, political intrigue, love and grief, and all-out war and senseless bloodshed.

Once you get up to speed with the political intricacies of the day, you'll be rewarded with a fast-paced, action-packed story.

Agent Strabo's Roman Mysteries

#1 Vox Populi

#2 Si Tacuisses

#3 Male Parta

#4 Quis Custodiet

#5 Non Omnia

#6 In Vino Veritas

About the Author

Alex is a former corporate business executive with a love of history and its mysteries.

Cloistered in his (very) small Hong Kong apartment due to the long pandemic-driven lockdown, he decided to travel back in time to his beloved South-East Europe and explore its rich history.

Since then, Alex has authored several historical mystery, historical fiction, and alternate history books.

Printed in Great Britain
by Amazon